"I can only ask you to trust me," Gil said quietly. "I cannot tell you what brings me here, what business I have with Colonel Fury."

"There is no need to tell me," Rowena replied fiercely. "You are here to try to bribe him to leave England because you fear what may come to light if he is brought to trial. You wait now for him to return with his answer."

Gil leaned forward across the table with his hand on her wrist, but the gentle clasp had become a vise-like grip, and his eyes were narrowed and jewel-hard.

"So you know that, do you?" he said softly. "How much did you hear besides?"

"Enough to know that I am to be given no chance to betray you, or your outlaw comrade . . . and that you know how to bend me to your will. . . ."

Fawcett Crest Books
by Sylvia Thorpe:

BEGGAR ON HORSEBACK
BELOVED REBEL
CAPTAIN GALLANT
THE CHANGING TIDE
FAIR SHINE THE DAY
A FLASH OF SCARLET
THE GOLDEN PANTHER
THE HIGHWAYMAN
THE RELUCTANT ADVENTURESS
ROGUES' COVENANT
ROMANTIC LADY
THE SCANDALOUS LADY ROBIN
THE SCAPEGRACE
THE SCARLET DOMINO
THE SILVER NIGHTINGALE
SPRING WILL COME AGAIN
THE SWORD AND THE SHADOW
SWORD OF VENGEANCE
TARRINGTON CHASE

SYLVIA THORPE

The
HIGHWAYMAN

FAWCETT CREST • NEW YORK

THE HIGHWAYMAN

THIS BOOK CONTAINS THE COMPLETE TEXT OF
THE ORIGINAL HARDCOVER EDITION.

Published by Fawcett Crest Books, a unit of CBS
Publications, the Consumer Publishing Division of CBS
Inc., by arrangement with The Hutchinson Publishing
Group.

ISBN: 0-449-23695-1

Printed in the United States of America

10 9 8 7 6 5 4 3 2 1

The
HIGHWAYMAN

PROLOGUE

The Inn of the Seven Magpies

The heavy, slate-coloured storm clouds which had grown so swiftly out of the heat of the day hung low over the flat countryside. It was a wild, desolate place, a vast tract of sand and scrub where flocks of pitiful, hungry-looking sheep found meagre grazing, and the forbidding shapes of gibbets lifted their gaunt, hideously burdened arms. A barren land, rich only in those harvests gathered at pistol-point by hardy rogues whose lives were spent in the shadow of the gallows, for this was Hounslow Heath in the summer of 1668, and its name rang ominously in the ears of travellers rich and poor.

The Heath might have been designed by nature for the benefit of outlaws. Although so large that it could have swallowed an army, and uninhabited save for a few small hamlets and scattered inns, it lay only a short distance from London and was crossed by two of the four great highways radiating from the capital, the Bath road, and that which passed by way of Staines to Salisbury and Exeter. Small wonder, then, that it was the delight of highwaymen and the bane of all honest folk who were obliged to cross its inhospitable expanse.

The evil notoriety of the Heath had lately been increased by the activities of a particularly daring and ruthless highwayman who went by the name of Colonel Fury, but on that sultry afternoon, as young Peter Buckland spurred his horse eastwards along the Staines road, he was concerned more with the certainty of the coming storm than with the possibility of encountering a robber. The self-styled Colonel was said to be the leader of a considerable band of thieves, and master of a system of spies which kept him informed of all rich travellers entering his domain, but Mr. Buckland was inclined to view such stories with a measure of scepticism. Any man, he thought, who could choose for himself so flamboyant a title must be a braggart and a bully, deliberately fostering a fearsome reputation in order to make his robberies easier.

A flash of lightning, followed by a long roll of thunder, caused his horse to shy, and Peter muttered an oath. He soothed the animal, and looked about him in the hope of discovering shelter of some kind, for though he was in haste to reach London he had no intention of riding through the storm if any alternative offered. The Heath stretched vacant and uninviting upon every side, and in disgust and exasperation he cursed the accident which had that morning befallen his coach, and his own impulsive action in hiring a saddle-horse and pressing on alone, leaving coach and baggage to follow in the charge of his servants.

He had almost resigned himself to the unpleasant prospect of facing the storm in the open when suddenly his questing gaze sharpened. He closed his eyes against another dazzle of lightning, and then opened them again to peer hard in the direction of the thing which had caught his attention. He was not mistaken. Far away to the north a slender thread of smoke, pale against the lowering storm clouds, rose straight into the still air.

Without pausing to consider the wisdom of the action, he urged his horse away from the highway towards it. He rode hard, for the storm was now very close, and so came at length to a clump of trees, from the other side of which the smoke appeared to rise. Skirting the trees, over ground which sloped down to a shallow depression, he found himself on a rough track which meandered across the Heath. Between trees and track stood a house, with a weather-beaten sign hanging from a rusty bracket between two of the upper windows to indicate that it was an inn.

It was a low, sprawling building, timber-framed, with small, diamond-paned windows, and a tiled roof patched with lichen, and it crouched in the hollow like a hare in its form, as though hoping to escape the attention of passers-by. The door stood open, but there was no sound or movement without or within, and in the sultry stillness the place had a secretive and faintly sinister air.

Thunder rumbled again, almost overhead, and a few big spots of rain pattered down on to the dusty earth as Peter dismounted and tethered his horse to an iron ring in the wall. He glanced up at the inn sign, and though the device upon it had been faded by time and weather to a muted blur, he was able with difficulty to make out the words painted beneath—The Seven Magpies.

He rapped sharply on the open door with the handle of his whip, and then, when that brought no response, stepped within, shouting for the host. He found himself in a narrow, stone-flagged passage. To the right, an open door revealed a deserted tap-room with tables and stools of rough-hewn oak; a corresponding door on the left was shut, concealing whatever lay behind it; before him, the passage turned sharply to the left, and in the angle thus formed steep stairs curved up and out of sight. Peter had time to notice that, in contrast to its shabby exterior the place was clean and well kept, and then footsteps approached and a man came round the corner of the passage.

At first sight he seemed old, for his hair gleamed silvery and his shoulders were bowed, but a closer look informed Peter that this impression was false. The man was scarcely past middle age. It was something other than time which had whitened his hair and etched deep lines on his pleasant, careworn face.

"Your house is well hidden, my friend," Peter greeted him amiably. "Had I not glimpsed the smoke from your chimney, I must needs have faced the storm on the open road."

"It is not often, sir, that travellers turn aside from the highway to seek us out," the man replied, "but they who know the Heath well, know the Seven Magpies also." He paused, and Peter had the curious impression that the words were meant to convey a warning of some kind, but next moment the inn-keeper was asking, ordinarily enough: "How may I serve your Honour?"

"First by having my horse stabled, and then by bringing me a draught of ale to wash the dust from my throat."

"It shall be done at once, sir. Be pleased to step

within." He opened the door on the left, ushered his guest into a small, square parlour, and withdrew, closing the door softly behind him.

Peter stood looking about him. The room was low-roofed and rather dark. A table with a big elbow-chair at its head and benches along either side stood in the middle of the floor, while almost the whole length of the wall facing the door was occupied by a mighty fire-place. Wooden settles on each side of the hearth, a cupboard in one corner, and a massive chest against the wall opposite the window completed the furnishings, which might have been those of the parlour of any small country inn. The only unusual object was a rapier with a hilt of cut steel and a worn but highly polished leather scabbard, which hung on the wall above the fireplace.

Peter walked across the room to examine the sword more closely, and acting upon a sudden impulse of curiosity, reached up to draw it a few inches from its sheath. The slender, three-sided blade gleamed sharp and deadly in another flicker of lightning, and with a frown he thrust it back and turned to survey the room again, conscious of a growing mystification. That sword was no mere ornament left to rust uncared-for, and the inn-keeper, though in appearance little different from any other, spoke with the voice of an educated man. The inn of the Seven Magpies, it seemed, was less commonplace than it at first appeared.

He moved back to the middle of the room, pulling off his gloves and flicking some of the dust from his dark blue camlet coat. The interior of the thick-walled inn seemed cool after the oppressive heat out on the Heath, but his lace cravat still felt uncomfortably tight, and the curls of the periwig lay hot and heavy across his shoulders. He dropped sprawling into the big chair and watched the rain quickening to a downpour beyond the tiny, deep-set window.

The clamour of the storm was now directly overhead, contrasting oddly with the unnatural silence within the house, but once he heard outside a clatter of hoofbeats which receded rapidly into the distance. It seemed strange that anyone should ride out in such weather, but his surprise was soon swallowed by a rising irritation. The minutes were passing and no one had come to attend to his needs, or to bring the ale for which his parched throat craved.

He was on the point of striding out to make his displeasure known when at last the door opened, and a young girl came in carrying a foaming tankard. The impatient words died on Peter's lips and he sat staring, for though she was dressed like any serving-maid, in a home-spun gown, and apron and close cap of coarse linen, there was a grace in her bearing which lent dignity to the simple garb, and her face had a delicate, flower-like prettiness which was unexpectedly refined. She set the tankard before him and was turning away again when he spoke quickly to detain her.

"Has my horse been cared for?"

"Aye, sir!" Her voice was soft and breathless, with none of the country broadness he had expected, but she did not look at him as she spoke. "Father saw to it himself."

"So!" Peter took a long pull at the ale, watching her over the rim of the pewter tankard. "How are you named, girl?"

"I am Patience, sir. Patience Birley."

"And it was your father who greeted me just now?"

"It was, your Honour."

There was a brief pause, while Peter took another drink, and the girl drew back towards the door, stealthily, as though she hoped he would not notice her retreat. Then he put the tankard down and said pleasantly:

"Well, Mistress Patience, you have few guests here, it seems! The place is more like a tomb than an inn."

"This is not the high-road, your Honour, and there's few like yourself, who turn aside to seek us out. Most folk cross the Heath as fast as may be."

"Thus, no doubt, showing their wisdom, for Hounslow Heath is no place for travellers to linger. Yet your father tells me that they who know it well, know this house also."

"Mayhap they do, sir!" She was at the door now, her hand upon the latch. "We have trade enough."

"So much that you must needs neglect the only guest at present beneath your roof?" He smiled as he spoke, but no response awoke in the girl's pale face. She stood with downcast eyes, one hand still on the door-latch, the other twisting at a fold of her apron. Peter tried again. "Tarry a moment! I have swallowed a deal of dust this day, and one draught of ale is not sufficient to quench my thirst. I will have you fill this tankard again."

"As your Honour pleases!" She waited, motionless, by the door until he held the empty vessel out to her, and then took it and went quickly from the room. Peter sat frowning, and wondering upon what manner of mystery he had stumbled, for with the appearance of Patience Birley his first, idle curiosity had deepened

13

into a resolve to probe further into this intriguing situation. The girl was plainly frightened, but he did not doubt his own ability to win her confidence.

When she returned with the tankard brimming again, he was ready, and as she placed it before him he put out his hand and grasped hers before she could move away, saying easily: "Bear me company awhile! 'Tis poor sport to sit and drink alone."

At his touch she froze into sudden stillness, neither responding nor trying to break away, but merely staring down at his hand clasped about her own. For a few seconds he studied her averted face, his gaze lingering appreciatively on the curve of her cheek and the strands of pale gold hair straying from beneath the close white cap. Then, as he sought to draw her nearer, she looked fully at him for the first time, and the terrified entreaty in her eyes struck him like a blow. Beneath the shock of it, his hold upon her slackened, and in an instant she had pulled herself free and fled from the room.

Peter stared after her in astonishment and some degree of chagrin, for tavern-girls were not generally remarkable for their prudery, and though he was not unduly vain he had expected no more than a brief pretence of reluctance. No woman had ever looked at him as Patience Birley had looked just now, and that she had done so was a considerable blow to his pride.

For a few minutes, injured self-esteem occupied his mind to the exclusion of all else, and then slowly the thought intruded that, just as this was no common inn, so Patience was no common servant-girl, and he was perhaps wrong to judge her by commonplace standards. For a moment or two he toyed with the notion that her present garb was some sort of masquerade, but after a little thought he rejected the possibility. Her looks and manner hinted at gentle birth, but the hand which he had held for a moment, though small and shapely, was roughened by much hard work. Whatever the truth about her, Patience Birley was no lady of quality in disguise.

With her departure, silence had settled again upon the house, nor did any other sound occur to break it. Peter sat drinking his ale and pondering the whole strange affair, while the storm crashed and rumbled overhead and finally rolled away into the distance. When he saw that the rain had stopped, he got up and went to open the door. The passage and the tap-room beyond were still empty.

"Ho, there!" he shouted. "The reckoning, if you please, and my horse to the door!"

He waited for a moment and then went back into the room, leaving the door wide. He expected the innkeeper himself to answer the summons, but to his surprise it was the girl's light step which presently approached. Entering, she closed the door and leaned her shoulders against it, staring across at him where he stood by the table.

"The storm has passed," he said after a moment. "I must be on my way if I am to reach London before dark."

She did not reply at once, but moved slowly towards him, as though each step were taken against her will yet under some compulsion too powerful to resist. Not until she stood, with downcast eyes, close beside him, did she speak, and then she said in a low voice:

"What need for haste, sir? I pray you, tarry here till

morning."

The words, and the tone in which they were uttered, held an invitation too plain to be misread, and he was conscious of a sharp, irrational disappointment. So she was like any other tavern-wench after all, and her earlier shrinking merely a pose to make him the more eager. He gave a short laugh, a sound full of contempt both for himself and for her, and pulled her into his arms, handling her more roughly than he would otherwise have done.

She remained passive in his embrace, her lips cold and unresponsive beneath his, and he became aware, in her complete lack of either response or withdrawal, of a kind of frozen calm which could spring only from the uttermost dispair. His perplexity returned, bringing compassion with it, and his grip upon her slackened until he merely held her lightly by the arms.

"You do this against your will," he said quietly. "If you fear me so greatly, why bid me to stay?"

She did not speak, or raise her eyes, but began to tremble as though in mortal peril. He hazarded another guess.

"Is it your father you fear? Does he force you to it?" Wordlessly she shook her head, and his hands tightened a little as he said more insistently: "Who, then, or what? Devil take it! I am not so great a villain that I would deny you aid or protection should you stand in need of it."

At last, slowly, she lifted her head to look at him, her blue eyes dazed and incredulous, and Peter was forcibly reminded of some small creature, a puppy or a kitten, so accustomed to ill-usage that kindness was unbelievable. She said in a whisper:

"You offer me your aid? You, a stranger?"

"Aye, gladly!" Peter was shaken by compassion, and by a tenderness new in his experience. "Nor will I ask anything in return. On my life, I swear it!"

For a long moment they regarded each other, and then she gave a sob and covered her face with her hands. Through her fingers, her voice came muffled.

"I cannot do it! God help me, I cannot do it!" It was a cry of desperation, but before he could ask its meaning, or even wonder at it, she was looking up at him again, her hands clutching urgently at the front of his coat.

"You must not linger! There is danger which grows greater with every moment you delay. I was meant to keep you here, but you have been kind and I will have no part in it! Come with me, quickly, and I will show you where your horse is stabled."

Without waiting for a reply, she caught him by the hand and led him out by the same way he had entered. Skirting the house, they crossed a cobbled yard to a fair-sized stable, empty save for Peter's horse, and there Patience turned to face him. Some of her timidity had vanished, and, for the present at least, she seemed buoyed up by a reckless courage.

"Ask me no questions, for the love of pity," she said in a low voice, "but get you gone, and do not draw rein until you are safe in Hounslow town. The saddle and bridle are yonder! See, I will help you, but hasten, hasten!"

Still mystified, but infected by a sense of urgency, he did as he was bidden, and between them the task was accomplished and the horse led out into the yard.

Patience pointed to the track which wound its way across the Heath.

"Follow that southwards and it will bring you to the high-road," she said hurriedly. "Now go, and pray, as I shall, that I have found my courage in time to save you."

His hand on the bridle, Peter regarded her with troubled eyes. "I am not certain from what danger you seek to shield me, but whatever it may be, I would rather stay to meet it than that you should come to harm for warning me of it."

She shook her head, and he saw in her eyes a sadness and a resignation that tugged at his heart. "To stay would cost you your life and profit me not at all, for I am beyond any man's aid. But you were willing to help me, and that means more to me than you can tell. I shall never forget it." She hesitated, and then added shyly, "Will you tell me your name?"

"It is Peter Buckland."

"I shall remember it." She smiled tremulously, and put out her hand to him. "God protect you, Peter!"

He took the hand in his own free one, reluctant to leave her, yet knowing that if the danger she spoke of was what he suspected, he would have little hope of defending her from it. Hating his own helplessness, he said in a low voice:

"May He protect you also, Patience," and bent to kiss her again, but gently this time, with tenderness and regret. Then he mounted and spurred away, and Patience stood gazing after him until horse and rider had vanished into the desolate spaces of the Heath.

The track which passed the door of the Seven Magpies twisted and turned, sometimes plainly marked, at others almost lost amid the rough, stony earth and tangled thickets, but it bore steadily towards the south, and at length Peter found himself once more upon the highway. The canopy of storm-cloud was broken and tattered now, but the light which streamed through it to gleam and fade across the barren waste was the red light of sunset. The road stretched empty and deserted, for only the reckless or those driven by urgent necessity risked life and property on Hounslow Heath when night was falling.

In spite of Patience Birley's insistence upon the need for haste, he allowed his horse's pace to slacken while he reflected upon his recent curious adventure. It was not difficult to guess the nature of the peril he had escaped. Numberless highwaymen infested the Heath, and a house such as the Seven Magpies, isolated, and yet conveniently placed between the two great roads, would provide an excellent stronghold. All this was commonplace enough. What was not commonplace was the unmistakable air of gentility which clung to Patience and her father, and the blind, despairing terror which seemed to possess the girl. He could not rid himself of the memory of it, and, even as he rode away from the inn, the conviction was growing in his mind that he would return.

He had reached a point where the road sloped gently upwards to a slight eminence crowned by one of the gibbets which disfigured the Heath. The ground on either side of the road was scattered with clumps of tall bushes, and when two horsemen materialised from among these and swept down upon him, Peter, still deep in thought, was taken by surprise. A shot whistled over his head, his horse shied wildly, and by the time he had regained control over it he was being covered by two long-barrelled pistols, and the chance to draw his own weapons had been lost.

For a few tense seconds, hunters and quarry regarded each other in silence. Only one of the highwaymen, the smaller and shabbier of the two, was masked. The other, a big man in claret-coloured velvet and a plumed hat, went arrogantly with his face uncovered, a swarthy, sensual face with a cruel mouth. He was richly dressed, and armed, in addition to his pistols, with a sword slung from an embroidered baldrick. He was the first to speak.

"Is this the man?" The words, addressed to his companion, were spoken in a harsh but not unpleasing voice which accorded well with his appearance.

"That it be, Colonel!" This was a boy's voice, betraying the speaker's youth. "I saw him plain when he rode up to the inn."

"But not when he rode away!" The Colonel's voice was charged with mockery, and so was the glance which he turned upon Peter. " 'Twas churlish of you, sir, not to tarry till I came, for did I not know the Heath so well that I can cross it without the aid of road or track, I might well have been denied the pleasure of your acquaintance."

Peter glared at him, torn between anger and misgiving. "Are you that braggart bully who styles himself 'Colonel Fury'?"

The highwayman laughed, but there was menace in the sound. "The cockerel crows loudly!" he remarked. "Yes, my friend, I am Colonel Fury, and you have put me to a deal of trouble this day. For that I claim payment. Yield up to my man whatever valuables you carry."

Before the unwavering menace of the pistol, Peter obeyed, and saw his purse, his watch and the diamond ring from his finger vanish into the younger highwayman's capacious pockets. He scarcely heeded the loss. Colonel Fury's words made it plain that they had come from the Seven Magpies, and concern for the girl outweighed momentarily his own danger.

"The horse also," the big man added. "Dismount, my friend!"

Seething but helpless, Peter obeyed. He was consumed by anxiety for Patience, but uncertain how much the highwayman knew or guessed, dared not voice a question for fear of implicating her in his flight. Fury's next words, however, revealed that he was aware of her part in it. Looking down at Peter as he stood angrily confronting him, the Colonel said with a sneer:

"So much for payment, but the score is not settled yet! Observe this fine gentleman, Thomas! Look well at him! This is the handsome spark who caused Mistress Patience to forget her obedience to me."

His henchman sniggered. "I'll wager, Colonel, she don't forget it again, not for many a day!"

Peter, conscious of an even deeper misgiving, took a pace forward, saying sharply: "Your decoy is not to blame, curse you! I am awaited in London, and no persuasion she could offer was potent enough to delay me."

"This is a most chivalrous gallant!" Fury remarked jeeringly. "You see, Thomas, how he lies to protect the wench. Spare your pains, my friend! That treacherous vixen has already felt the weight of my whip, for I allow no doxy of mine to flout me."

Peter glanced at the heavy riding-whip the highwayman carried, and an appalling picture of Patience cowering beneath its cruel lash formed in his mind. Reckless of the consequences, he said in a voice unsteady with anger:

"Damned ruffian! 'Tis easy to be bold with women, or with a man whom you hold at pistol-point, but 'tis plain you have no more stomach to use that sword you bear than you have right to wear it!"

The mocking grin vanished from Fury's face and his lips tightened to a thin, cruel line. For a second or two he pondered the younger man, his eyes bright and cold with a deadly anger, and then he swung out of the saddle to confront him. Very deliberately he raised his pistol and set its muzzle against Peter's chest.

"I have both," he said softly, "and I stand in no need of proving my mettle against a bearless boy. Turn now, and walk where I bid you." To Thomas he flung a brief command. "Bring the horses."

"Colonel, this be folly!" the boy protested uneasily. "In God's name, make an end, and let's be gone!"

"Do as I bid you. This whelp needs schooling!" To Peter he added: "Walk, my friend!"

So, with Thomas and the horses trailing after them, they came to the crest of the rise, and faced each other again at the very foot of the gibbet, with the chained and shrunken corpse swinging above. Peter glanced up at it, and then at the man before him.

"I will remember you, Colonel Fury," he said in a tone of concentrated anger, "and as God is my witness, I will see you hang as high as this rogue above us."

22

Fury laughed. "I would not take a wager upon that, my young friend," he replied threateningly, "but you *will* remember me. Yes, by God, you will remember me until you draw your last breath!" Over his shoulder he added: "Thomas, tether the horses, and then cut me a good length of strap from the bridle of the spare beast."

In silence and some haste Thomas obeyed, apparently anxious to see completed whatever grim business his leader had in mind. Peter waited with outward calm, scorning to betray the uneasiness which was growing within him. He had courage enough, but neither the place nor the hour was conducive to boldness. The chains holding the corpse rattled in a sudden breeze, and a shaft of sunset-light, thrusting between the torn clouds, bathed the whole scene for a few moments in a baleful glow.

Thomas brought the length of strap, and once again Peter was ordered to turn. He felt the muzzle of the pistol cold against the nape of his neck as Thomas, at Colonel Fury's command, jerked his arms above his head and lashed his wrists fast to the gibbet-post. Then the weapon was withdrawn, to be replaced a moment later by a sharp knife-blade; cloth ripped, and he felt the rain-freshened air cool upon his shoulders.

"Now, my bold gallant," said Fury's hateful voice, "we come to the lesson which will impress me so firmly upon your memory."

Peter, realising his purpose, braced himself to resist it, but in spite of his resolution he gasped and flinched when the lash of the whip seared like flame across his naked back. Again and again it fell, until the whole world reeled crazily in a mist of white-hot agony, and all his attention must be focused upon the effort needed not to cry out.

At last came a merciful cessation of the blows, and then, through weakness and the clamouring pain, he became aware of the highwayman still close beside him, heard again the harsh, taunting voice:

"The wind freshens and grows chill, and darkness promises to bring more rain with it. There will be no travellers abroad tonight to succour you, so ponder your own folly until I come again. I will return at daybreak."

He paused, as though awaiting a reply, but Peter was beyond speech, almost beyond coherent thought, and with a short, contemptuous laugh Colonel Fury turned and left him. As though from a great distance, Peter heard the horses move away, the sound of their hoof-beats growing fainter and fading gradually into silence. He was alone upon the darkening Heath, and he knew that even if he survived the night, sentence of death had already been passed upon him. His head sank forward; the iron casing of the gibbet-post was cold against his cheek, and above him the bones of the dead man shook in the rising wind.

1

The Messenger

At Peter Buckland's house in Westminster, his sister Rowena had awaited his coming throughout the sultry summer day. At first with eagerness, then with impatience, and finally, as evening closed in, with anger and disappointment. It was her twentieth birthday, and before Peter had left her to visit friends in Berkshire, he had promised to return in time to spend it with her. She had not doubted his word, and had even toyed with the idea of giving in to him upon a matter which for months had been a source of disagreement between them, but when it became obvious that he would not return that day, she suffered an abrupt change of heart. Let him do what he might, she would never obey him now, and to strengthen that resolve she declared it to the impoverished, widowed cousin who was her companion and duenna.

Mrs. Marriott, an elderly lady as timid and colourless as Rowena was forthright and headstrong, looked at her with profound dismay. It was her belief that a woman should always defer without question to the wishes of the head of the family, even when, as in this instance, he happened to be a brother less than two years the elder.

"I beg of you, Rowena, do not allow your present ill-humour to cause a lasting breach between you and your brother," she said earnestly. "It may be that he is in no way to blame for failing to keep his word. There are so many trifling accidents which could have delayed him."

"Had he set forth in good time, he would have been here today in spite of any delays," Rowena replied inexorably. "No, you may depend that he has found better entertainment at his friend's house in Berkshire than that of bearing his sister company upon her birthday."

"Young men are ever heedless," Mrs. Marriott remarked diffidently, "but Peter is devoted to you, there is no doubt."

Rowena gave a scornful laugh. "So devoted, in fact, that for the better part of a year he has sought to bully me into a marriage which I regard with the utmost repugnance. Well, he will not succeed! His neglect of me today has set the seal upon that!"

"But, my child, you *must* marry! It is little short of scandalous that a woman as well dowered as yourself should reach her twentieth birthday still unwed."

Rowena's face clouded and she was silent for a moment. Then she said quietly: "It is no fault of mine, cousin, that I have done so. I would have been very happy to make the marriage my father had arranged for me, but God willed otherwise."

Mrs. Marriott sighed, for there was no denying that Rowena had been unfortunate. Betrothed at thirteen to Ranulf Elland, a gentleman of some consequence in their native Leicestershire, she had seen her marriage delayed first by the death of her father, and then, within a year, of her mother. She was nearly seventeen before preparations for the wedding could be made, and when they were almost complete her bridegroom fell victim to the dreaded smallpox. Mrs. Marriott had been with her then, and had realised that, to Rowena, the third blow had been the bitterest of all.

"It is not for us to question His purposes, Rowena," she said gently. "I know how deeply you grieved for Mr. Elland, but that was three years ago. It is not right that the young should mourn for ever."

"Ranulf meant so much to me!" Rowena laid down the embroidery upon which she had been engaged, and rested her head aginst the back of the chair; her voice was dreamy. "All through those years when my father was in exile and our home in the hands of strangers, and my mother and Peter and I lived at Elland Manor, it was to Ranulf we all turned in time of need. He was a grown man and I still in the nursery, but he was never too busy to help and guide me. We all depended upon him, even my father when he returned to England with the King. We all needed him!"

Mrs. Marriott nodded. King Charles had restored to the elder Peter Buckland the estate which had been taken from him, but he could not restore the health shattered by nearly twenty years of war and poverty and exile. Buckland had come home a dying man, and Mrs. Marriott, who had gone to live with her kinsfolk after her own husband's death, had seen how quickly he learned to rely upon young Elland's self-assurance and knowledge of local matters. A staunch Royalist herself, she had wondered a little that a man who had given so much to the Royal cause could contemplate giving his only daughter to one who, by steering a discreetly moderate course, had succeeded in maintaining intact his lands and fortune. The widow had not greatly liked Ranulf Elland, but she reminded herself that her kinsman's debt of gratitude to him was very great. It would have fared ill with Mrs. Buckland and the children if Elland had not taken them under his protection.

"You are mistaken in thinking, however, that I still grieve for Ranulf," Rowena went on after a moment. "Time has healed that wound, and I can think of him now with affection, and no pain. But I will not dishonour his memory by giving myself in marriage to a man as godless and dissolute as he was honourable and kind."

These were strong words, and they goaded Mrs. Marriott to unwonted protest. Usually, overborne by the younger woman's stronger character, she kept her opinions to herself, but now she said in what, for her, amounted to a tone of sharp rebuke:

"That is no way to speak of your brother's closest friend! What is more, you speak without authority or knowledge, since as yet you are scarcely acquainted with Sir Gilroy Mabyn."

"Nor have I any desire to be." Rowena replied scornfully. "As for knowledge, Sir Gilroy's name is a byword."

"Gossip, and malicious gossip at that!" Mrs. Marriott retorted boldly. "He is no worse than any other gentleman at Court, and far better than many."

"No worse than my Lord Rochester, or the Duke of Buckingham, or the rest of the Court rakes," Rowena replied contemptuously. "That, madam, is small recommendation!"

"Your brother has set his heart upon this marriage."

"He will not force me to it against my will," Rowena said confidently. "For all his talk of compelling me to obey him, he has too great an affection for me deliberately to make me unhappy."

"Perhaps he will not force you to make *this* marriage," Mrs. Marriott reminded her, "but he may well forbid you to contract any other. Is it possible that, being offered a choice between becoming my Lady Mabyn, and remaining a spinster, you would choose the latter?"

"Indeed I would!" Rowena lifted her chin defiantly. "Better by far to live unwed than with a husband from whom I could expect neither consideration nor faithfulness!"

Mrs. Marriott shook her head. "Such words do not become you to utter, nor me to hear," she said severely. "Have you given no thought to the unenviable position which will be yours when Peter marries, as he is bound to do? You will not be mistress of his household then! You will have no choice but to give up your place to his wife, not only here, but at Mereworth also."

"Mereworth!" Rowena spoke the name with a sigh, and, putting aside her sewing, got up and went to stand by the window. "Ah, cousin, you do not know the homesickness that thought arouses in me. Peter may love London, but I wearied of it long since. I wish I could return to Mereworth! I wish I had never been persuaded to leave it!"

Mrs. Marriott sighed also, but for a different reason.

29

She was deeply attached to her young kinswoman, but she could not deny that Rowena was both wilful and stubborn. Studying her now as she stood by the window, she thought how regrettable it was that a young woman so amply blessed in other respects should possess two such grave flaws in her character. Rowena was well-born, well-educated, and, thanks to the careful provisions of her father's Will, provided with an ample income. She had even been granted good looks, for though she was perhaps a trifle too tall and slender in an age when the ideal of feminine beauty was an opulent plumpness, this fault was balanced by the fine hazel eyes, clear skin and abundant, chestnut-coloured hair which both she and Peter had inherited from their mother. They were, in fact, strikingly alike, in temperament as well as in looks. Both were impulsive and headstrong, with tempers which flared quickly and died as soon, and both were more easily led than driven.

Therein, Mrs. Marriott reflected shrewdly, lay the cause of much of the present discord between them. If Peter had been less eager to thrust his friend, Sir Gilroy Mabyn, upon his sister as soon as she came to join him in London, and Rowena prepared to admit that the dead Ranulf was not, perhaps, the only man she could ever admire; if Peter had waited a little longer before mentioning the subject of marriage, or even pretended that such an alliance would be displeasing to him, the whole affair might have been happily concluded by now. Mrs. Marriott suspected that Sir Gilroy was well able to conduct his courtship without any aid or advice from the lady's brother. His conquests were many, and she could not understand how Rowena could remain indifferent to a charm of which even the widow herself had been instantly aware.

She knew better, however, than to put these thoughts into words, and contented herself instead with trying to find excuses for the absent Peter, and to soothe Rowena's ruffled temper. Neither effort was successful, and the two ladies finally wished each other goodnight in an atmosphere of distinct chilliness.

Early the following morning Rowena was awakened by her maid, and blinking the mists of sleep from eyes and brain, saw that the woman was herself only half-dressed and that she carried a folded paper in her hand. Chilled by a vague foreboding, Rowena sat up and put out her hand for it, while the maid stammered excuse and explanation. The letter had been brought to the house during the night with the command that it be delivered immediately to Miss Buckland, but the porter who kept the gate had been reluctant to rouse the household. As soon as the servants were astir, however, he had consulted with them, and it was decided that the letter should be given to their mistress without further delay.

Rowena listened in silence, turning the sealed paper over in her hand. Her name was inscribed upon it in a writing she did not recognise, but which contrasted strongly with the indifferent quality of the paper. Frowning, she broke the seal, and, looking first for a signature, could find none. The message informed her, in the same flowing hand and with a courtly turn of phrase, that her brother had met with an accident and now lay injured at a cottage on the edge of Hounslow Heath. This was followed by directions how to find the place, and a courteous apology for being the bearer of such ill tidings, but there was no clue whatsoever to the identity of the writer. Rowena read it through twice in growing dismay, and then said sharply to the maid:

"Bid Master Thorne come to me as soon as may be, and then come back and help me to dress. And hasten, girl, hasten!"

The woman, looking frightened, hurried out, and Rowena rose quickly from the bed. Her maid soon returned, and by the time that a tap on the door heralded the arrival of the Bucklands' oldest and most trusted servant, Rowena was fully clad and seated before her dressing-table while her hair was arranged in the elaborate fashion of the day.

Tobias Thorne, a tall, lean man who walked with a pronounced limp, had served the Buckland family for thirty of his forty-five years, and now occupied in the household a position of singular trust and privilege. His lameness had prevented him from following his late master to the wars, and Rowena had therefore seen him almost every day of her life, so that to her, as to her brother, he was far more a friend than a servant. During the past few months, his approval of Sir Gilroy Mabyn and his blunt expression of it had caused Rowena some displeasure, but now she had no hesitation in turning to him for advice. Holding the letter out to him, she said without preamble:

"What think you of this? Are we to believe the news it brings?"

Tobias took the paper and read it through before he spoke. Then he said slowly:

"To my mind, Miss Rowena, we have no choice but to believe it. If 'tis true, then Mr. Peter is in sore need of help. You did look to see him yesterday, did you not?"

She nodded. "I did, and now I am ashamed of the uncharitable thoughts I harboured when he did not come. Oh, Tobias, we must go to him with all speed! Have my coach made ready at once."

"I'll see to it, Miss Rowena, and I'll see to it also that we go in such strength that if this letter be a trick of some sort, you'll come to no harm through it. It seems the porter can tell us nothing of the man who delivered it, for 'twas dark, and he kept his hat pulled down over his face. But he spoke like a gentleman, and 'twould not be the first time some young spark had used a ruse such as this to carry off a maid who took his fancy."

As he had expected, Rowena brushed this possibility impatiently aside, merely bidding him make what arrangements he liked for the journey, as long as he made them quickly. Tobias hurried off to do so, and Rowena, summoning Mrs. Marriott, showed her the letter and told her to make preparations to receive a sick man. Then, paying no heed to the duenna's protests and lamentations, she flung a wrap around her shoulders and hurried out to the waiting coach. Tobias and two mounted grooms were ready to accompany her, and both they and the coachman were heavily armed.

The directions given by their unknown informant were easy enough to follow, and they reached their destination without difficulty. It was a labourer's cottage at the end of a straggling hamlet, with the bleak expanse of Hounslow Heath stretching beyond, and Rowena watched anxiously from the coach as Tobias limped along the path and rapped on the open door. After a moment a young woman with a baby in her arms and an older child clinging to her skirts came to the threshold. A brief conversation followed, and then Tobias returned to the coach.

"The letter spoke truth, Miss Rowena," he said grimly. "Your brother is within."

He helped her to alight, and followed her along the rough path to where the young woman waited in the doorway. She curtsied as Rowena reached her, and said timidly:

"The young gentleman be sleeping now, madam, but if ye'll step within, I'll take 'ee to him."

Rowena nodded and followed her into the house, her silken skirts sweeping across the bare earthen floor. The woman led her to an inner room, where upon a rough pallet bed Peter lay prone, covered by a thread-bare blanket. His great periwig had been removed along with his upper garments, and without it he looked curiously young and defenceless. Standing beside the pallet, his sister said softly:

"What is the nature of his injury?"

For answer the woman bent down and with her free hand drew the blanket gently aside, revealing a back bruised and lacerated from shoulders to waist. Rowena drew a sharp, horrified breath.

"Who dared to do this thing?" she asked passionately.

"Madam, the gentleman spoke of Colonel Fury."

"The highwayman?" Rowena whispered, and behind her, Tobias cursed softly. "But why? Was not robbery enough?"

The other woman shook her head, and glanced fearfully over her shoulder as though she half expected to see Fury himself standing there, conjured up by the mere mention of his name. Then Peter stirred and groaned and muttered something unintelligible, and Rowena dropped to her knees beside him.

" 'Tis I, Rowena," she said softly, laying her hand on his hair. "Be easy, my dearest brother! I have come to take you home."

He did not seem to hear her, but again muttered a few disjointed phrases, and this time she was able to distinguish the words.

"Patience . . . the Seven Magpies! Patience!" A pause, and then, more distinctly: "I will remember you, Colonel Fury!"

Rowena's hand moved to touch his cheek, and found it burning beneath her fingers. She looked up in dismay at her companions.

"The fever is upon him," she said in a low voice. "Tobias, what are we to do?"

"Best bear him home, as you intended. He will do better in his own bed. I'll summon the others, and we'll carry him out to the coach." He smiled reassuringly into her worried eyes. "Don't fret now, Miss Rowena! Can you not trust me to look after you both?"

"Have you not always done so?" she countered with a faint smile. "Go then, Tobias! Do as you think best."

So presently Peter was borne out to the coach, while his sister, who had gone back to the outer room, turned to the woman of the house.

"You have my deepest gratitude," she said quietly, "for my brother is very dear to me. Now tell me, I pray you, how he came here."

The young woman hesitated, shifting the baby's

weight to the other arm, her eyes not meeting Rowena's. At length she said:

"He were brought to us by a stranger who found him out on the Heath, bound to a gibbet-post and nigh crazed wi' pain. He set him free and took him up on his horse, and this were the first house he chanced on."

Rowena looked at her, a faint frown in her eyes. "Then it was this stranger who brought me word of my brother's plight? But how did he know his name, and where he dwelt?"

"Madam, the young gentleman were able to tell us that himself, and the other man said he were bound for London, and would bear the news."

"I see!" Rowena spoke thoughtfully. "What was he like, this kindly stranger?"

Again there was a palpable hesitation before the woman replied. "Madam, I paid no heed to his looks. Your brother, poor young gentleman, needed all my care."

Rowena could think of nothing else to say. She felt certain that the woman was lying, but it would be rank ingratitude to challenge her, since it was plain that she and the mysterious stranger had between them saved Peter's life. So she sighed, and, taking out some pieces of gold, laid them on the rough wooden table in the middle of the room.

"Pray accept this as a token of my gratitude," she said quietly. "As for the stranger who brought my brother to you, I must pray that Heaven will reward him, since it seems that I cannot."

2

Rowena

The question of the mysterious rescuer continued to haunt Rowena's mind at intervals during the next few days, but for the most part her thoughts were wholly concerned with her brother. He suffered considerably during the journey back to London, in spite of all that she could do to spare him, and by nightfall his fever was high enough to cause her some anxiety. She summoned the best physician she could discover and herself nursed Peter devotedly, and had her reward in the fact that within a week the fever had subsided and the marks of the whip begun to heal.

Meanwhile, news of his misadventure had spread through the town. Recounted in the first place to their equals by servants furious at the outrage upon their young master, it soon reached the ears of those of higher degree, and messages of inquiry and good wishes began to pour in, for Peter Buckland was a popular young man.

One of the earliest and most persistent callers was Sir Gilroy Mabyn, but Rowena, making attendance upon her brother the excuse, declined to see him, and instead sent Mrs. Marriott with formal expressions of reassurance, and thanks for his solicitude. To another visitor, a serious young man named John Somerton who also aspired to her hand, she was more gracious. She spent half an hour in his company, and drew a good deal of satisfaction from the thought of the annoyance which this would cause Sir Gilroy if he ever heard of it.

As soon as Peter felt well enough to receive visitors, however, it was Sir Gilroy whom he expressed an urgent desire to see. Observing the expression of faint distaste with which his sister greeted this, he was moved to add irritably:

"No need to show me that disdainful face! What the plague ails you that you dislike Gil Mabyn so?"

"Do not distress yourself, my dear," she replied soothingly, paying no heed to the question. "You shall see Sir Gilroy when next he comes here, that I promise you."

"I warrant I will!" Peter spoke belligerently, for he had reached that stage of recovery where he was decidedly short-tempered. "And you will favour me, Rowena, by making him welcome."

"It is my hope," she retorted a trifle sharply, "that I never treat any guest in this house with less than courtesy."

"There's a deal of difference between courtesy and cordiality," her brother observed shrewdly, "and I have yet to see you bestow the latter upon Gil. No, all your smiles are reserved for that dull dog, Somerton. 'Tis sheer perversity, for Gil Mabyn is worth a dozen of him!"

"Mr. Somerton is a man of sense and worth," Rowena said heatedly, "and though his conversation be sober, it is a pleasant change from endless levity and malicious gossip. I might like Sir Gilroy better if he possessed a little of John Somerton's dignity and moderation. It would be more becoming in a man of his years and position."

Peter gave a short, angry laugh. "A man of his years!" he repeated scornfully. "Gil is but six-and-twenty. You speak of him as though he were a grey-beard."

"And he behaves as irresponsibly as a schoolboy," she retorted with spirit. "He is for ever involved in some mad prank!"

"As when he sailed as gentleman-volunteer against the Dutch," Peter said sarcastically. "Venturing his life when so many of us bided safe at home! Irresponsible indeed!"

"I cast no doubt upon Sir Gilroy's courage," she said more equably, "but are you trying to tell me that he was fired by some high ideal of patriotism when he joined the fleet?"

For a moment her brother continued to glare at her, and then his sense of humour came to his aid. "Would that I could," he said ruefully, "since it might persuade you to regard him more kindly, but Gil himself would be the first to deny it. I believe he volunteered from sheer love of adventure, and because he was weary of Court life."

"Because he had fallen into disfavour with the King," Rowena corrected him scornfully. "Oh, Peter, I am out of all patience with you! Why do you regard Sir Gilroy Mabyn as an example to be admired and followed, when all the world knows that he is nothing more than an idle, dissolute libertine?"

Peter heaved himself upright against his pillows, and cursed as the movement irked his tender back and shoulders.

"The world, as usual, fancies that it knows a deal more than it does," he said angrily, "and you never pause to consider that my knowledge and judgment of Gil is perhaps more trustworthy than the gossip you affect to despise. Now attend to me, Rowena! You know my wishes where you and Gil Mabyn are concerned, and I will not wait for ever to see them gratified. He has been uncommon patient as it is!"

Rowena took a turn about the room in the hope of soothing her ruffled feelings, and then halted again beside her brother's bed. "Mr. Somerton has also expressed a desire to marry me," she reminded him. "I know that you are right in urging me to wed, but why cannot my preferences be considered?"

"Because Gil is by far the better match," Peter said bluntly. "His estate and fortune are twice the size of Somerton's, and there's the title besides. What is more, as I told you just now, he is the better man."

"So you tell me continuously," she replied scornfully. "I cannot agree!"

"You are in no position to judge," Peter retorted. "Let me tell you that you should consider yourself fortunate. You are the first woman to whom Gil has offered marriage, and there are many who would be more than willing to become his wife."

"I have heard that many have done so, in everything but name!" Rowena's tone was contemptuous. "From Maids of Honour at Whitehall to actresses in Drury Lane. Sir Gilroy's conquests range wide!"

Peter grinned at her. "Can he be blamed for following a Royal example?" he remarked. "In any event, if you imagine that Somerton is some kind of saint, you are vastly mistaken. He is less successful than Gil in his amours, and more secretive, like the curst Puritan I suspect him of being, but that is the only difference between them."

Rowena, her cheeks flushed and her eyes sparkling with anger, sought for some adequate retort, and, finding none, glared at her brother in frustrated silence. He returned the regard with equal animosity.

"We will have no more argument," he announced loftily. "You will marry Gil Mabyn, and there's an end to it, so let me hear no more of your preference for Somerton. I know whence that springs, even though you do not admit as much. He sets you in mind of Ranulf."

For a few seconds Rowena continued to meet his eyes, and then her glance fell before his. She said in a low voice: "And if he does, is it any wonder that I prefer him to Sir Gilroy? I loved and respected Ranulf very dearly."

"Aye, as you loved and respected our father, whose place Ranulf filled for so many years," Peter replied shrewdly, "but 'tis of a husband we are speaking now, and not a parent. It is my belief that Gil will make you a better husband than ever Ranulf would have done."

"You never liked him!" Rowena's voice was bitter.

"No, I did not," Peter agreed flatly. "That is why at the first opportunity I came to London, where I might live to please myself and not as he thought fit to instruct me. I was not content, even if you were, to spend my life endeavouring to be that which I am not."

She looked up sharply. "That is untrue! All that

Ranulf sought to do was to help us, both of us, to overcome our faults."

"My faults are my own concern, and I will overcome them unaided, or not at all," Peter retorted bluntly. "Moreover, those things which in you he regarded as faults, to my mind are nothing of the kind. If he desired a meek and mouse-like bride, he should have sought one formed thus by nature." He leaned back against his pillows and regarded his sister in a baffled way. "Devil knows why you persist in clinging to the past in this fashion! Gil has wit enough to desire you as you are, so why can you not be equally content?"

With an inarticulate exclamation Rowena turned and ran from the room, slamming the door behind her. She fled to her bedchamber, and, having turned the key against possible intrusion by Mrs. Marriott, sat down before her dressing-table and tried to compose herself.

She was deeply agitated, for her brother's words had struck uncomfortably close to a truth which until that moment she had been reluctant to acknowledge. John Somerton did remind her of Ranulf. With him she felt safe, like a ship in a familiar harbour, with no need to face the unknown dangers of stormy, uncharted seas. Ranulf had deplored her fiery temper and the wilfulness which led her so often into trouble, and had sought, patiently and gently, to help her to curb them. He had never wholly succeeded, but he had implanted in her a feeling that spirit was undesirable in a woman, and that the future she desired was a peaceful, uneventful life as the wife of a sober country gentleman. Sir Gilroy Mabyn could certainly not offer her this, and so she had resisted the prospect of marriage to him with every means at her command from the moment it was first suggested to her. Much of her hard-won serenity and self-control had deserted her in the process, and she had no hesitation in laying the blame for this upon Sir Gilroy. She avoided him whenever possible, but even so, he seemed to have the power to arouse all those aspects of her nature which she had been taught to regard as the least admirable.

She rested her elbows on the table and her chin on her hands, staring at her reflection in the silver-framed mirror. The truth was that she found Sir Gilroy infinitely disturbing. With Mr. Somerton, as with other gentlemen of her acquaintance, she could be calm and confident, mistress of the situation and of her own emotions, but with him it was not so. He made her mistrust herself, and therefore she mistrusted him, and seized eagerly upon any scrap of gossip—and there were many—which seemed to confirm the low opinion of him which she was determined to hold.

When next she went to her brother's room, no mention was made of their dispute or of the man who was the cause of it, but on the following day, when Rowena, with her duenna in attendance, was once again entertaining John Somerton, a servant entered to announce the arrival of Sir Gilroy himself. Mr. Somerton was betrayed into showing a flicker of annoyance, but Rowena, though equally put out, calmly desired the lackey to admit the newcomer to her presence. She had no intention of failing to make good her boast that all guests, welcome or unwelcome, were received with courtesy, and assured herself that her only feeling at sight of this one was vexation.

In any company Gilroy Mabyn was a man difficult to overlook. Taller than most, and of a powerful build which not even the elaborately laced and beribboned fashions of the day could wholly disguise, he carried with him an air of boundless enthusiasm for life. He was not a particularly handsome man, but his lean face with its high cheekbones and humorous mouth was one which lingered in the memory when more classical features had been forgotten. He came into the room, Rowena thought furiously, like a conqueror entering a captured citadel, and the fancy lent a greater degree of coolness to her greeting. This did nothing to daunt Sir Gilroy. He took the hand which, with a distant air, she held out to him, but bent swiftly from his great height before she realised his intention, and kissed her on the lips.

She snatched her hand away and retreated a step, colour flaming across her face. Custom allowed the greeting-kiss, but he had never before claimed it, and she could not tell whether the thing were done on an impulse of devilment or prompted by her own coldness and his rival's presence, or as a subtle way of asserting his position as the suitor favoured by her brother. Nor did the gay mockery of his glance do anything to enlighten her. In complexion he was as dark as King Charles himself, yet beneath slanting black brows his eyes were a clear green-blue, startling as aquamarines in that swarthy face. They smiled down at her now as though he were aware of her confusion and amused by it, and this infuriated her even further.

"Miss Buckland is fortunate indeed," he remarked lightly. "Her frown is as becoming as other women's smiles."

"Did I frown upon you, Sir Gilroy?" Rowena had recovered swiftly, and though her colour was still high, her tone matched his for lightness. "That was not my intention. You are very welcome." His eyebrows lifted in mute disbelief, and she smiled sweetly up at him as she took her revenge. "My brother is much recovered, and craves entertainment. Most particularly has he asked for you, and I promised to apprise you of it. I pray you, go bear him company awhile."

She was obliged to admit that he took the dismissal well. His smile broadened a little in acknowledgment of her triumph, and he said pleasantly:

"To please you, madam, must always be my concern, and the task you set me now I shall perform most gladly. It is good news indeed that Peter mends fast."

Mr. Somerton decided that the time had come to assert himself. "Stern measures should be taken to rid Hounslow Heath of that rogue, Colonel Fury," he announced severely. " 'Tis scandalous that so monstrous a villain should swagger it unhindered upon our roads."

Sir Gilroy turned to regard him with an expression of mild surprise. He gave the impression that, until that moment, Mr. Somerton's presence in the room had escaped his attention.

"Easy to say, sir, but difficult to accomplish," he observed. "It is said that Colonel Fury surrounds himself with a veil of mystery. That none knows his real identity, and that his minions are everywhere, to give warning of any movement against him."

"Tomfoolery, sir!" Mr. Somerton declared brusquely. "Gossip fit for the ears of none but credulous fools! I'll wager that these tales of Fury's spies are as false as those which credit the rogue with gentle birth."

Sir Gilroy continued to smile, but there was more

than a hint of mockery in his face. "Be not so harsh in your judgment, Mr. Somerton," he said. "More than one gentleman has been glad to take to the highway when all other resources failed him. Who knows to what straits you or I may be reduced at some future time?"

Rowena, in some alarm, made haste to intervene. Somerton's face had darkened with anger, and she put no trust in Mabyn's forbearance, in spite of his pleasant looks. Signing discreetly to Mrs. Marriott to summon a servant, she said quickly:

"I pray you, gentlemen, let us have no more talk of Colonel Fury. I cannot hear his name without remembering the brutality with which he used my poor brother, and I pray that the day is not far distant when he will reap the reward he deserves. Until then, let us put him out of our minds."

She was thankful to see that her intervention had the desired effect, and she continued to chatter brightly until a servant appeared to conduct Sir Gilroy to Peter's room. When the door had closed behind the unpredictable guest she breathed a sigh of relief, and turned to resume her interrrupted discourse with Mr. Somerton. Yet somehow her earlier interest in it had vanished, and she was glad when some twenty minutes later he took his leave. It was all Sir Gilroy's fault, she reflected angrily. The interruption caused by his arrival and his conduct had put her out of tune with herself and everyone else.

For a little while longer she remained where she was, toying in a desultory fashion with her embroidery, and then she dismissed her companion and made her way towards her brother's room. Peter had enjoyed enough diversion for one day, she told herself as she went. He must not be allowed to overtax his strength.

Her hand was already upon the door of his room when she became aware that the voices within, her brother's, and Mabyn's deeper tones, did not sound like those of friends engaged in amiable conversation. She could not distinguish the words, but it was evident that the two men spoke in anger. She hesitated, unwilling to walk in upon a quarrel, and then Sir Gilroy's voice spoke just beyond the door, with a distinctness that made her jump.

". . . gave you good advice! Be guided by it, you hot-headed young fool, and concern yourself no more with the Seven Magpies."

It was plain that he was on the point of leaving the room, and Rowena, dismayed at the prospect of being found eavesdropping, fled on tiptoe along the corridor and dived behind the long curtains framing the window at its end. Peeping through the crack between wall and curtain, she saw Sir Gilroy emerge from Peter's room, closing the door with a quiet viciousness more ominous than violence, and stride past her on his way out of the house. His dark face was grimly set, the eyes which had smiled upon her so short a time ago were now hard and bright as jewels, and there was a kind of restrained fury in his every movement. Long after he had gone, Rowena remained in her hiding-place. She leaned trembling against the wall, and wondered with inexplicable dismay what had passed between the two men to set that look upon Gilroy Mabyn's face.

3

The Quest

She did not seek an explanation from Peter. She did
not even carry out her original intention of going to his
room, and when at length she did visit him again,
she waited in vain for him to make some reference to
Sir Gilroy's visit. Nor did he speak of it at all in the
days which followed. Rowena, perplexed and uneasy,
tried a score of times to broach the subject, but always
her courage failed her before the first word could be
uttered. Sir Gilroy did not approach her again, and
eventually she learned by chance from a mutual acquaintance that he had gone out of London.

She told herself that she was glad of it, and of the
sudden coolness between him and her brother, since
while it lasted there would presumably be no more
planning of marriages. Yet she could not entirely cast
off a feeling of uneasiness, an impression, so vague that
it could not be defined, that all was not as it should be.

Peter's attitude during the days of his recovery did
nothing to reassure her. He had become morose and
preoccupied, unwilling to discuss his misadventure, and
inclined to fly into a rage if she persisted in talking of

it. Rowena had shown him the letter she had received, and told him of her unrewarding talk with the young woman at the cottage, hoping that he might throw some light on the mystery, but he had merely glanced at the paper and then tossed it aside, declaring that he could remember nothing of his rescuer. Colonel Fury had stopped and robbed him, and then, because Peter had not betrayed the abject terror which the highwayman apparently regarded as his due, meted out to him the punishment of which she was aware. More than that he could not recall.

Rowena felt certain that he was concealing something, but though she would have given much to be taken into his confidence, she could understand his reluctance to talk of what had happened. To be robbed on the highway was nothing, and most travellers suffered it at one time or another, but to be stripped and flogged like a common criminal, by one who was himself outside the law, was a humiliation which had scarred Peter's pride more cruelly than Fury's whip had scarred his back. All London knew of the insult the highwayman had put upon him, but any expression of sympathy was rebuffed as brusquely as questions had been, and at length Rowena grew weary of attempting either. In his present mood Peter was best left alone.

None the less, she was considerably surprised when she returned to the house one day to be greeted by the news that Mr. Buckland had ridden out soon after her own departure. He had left a note for her, but this merely stated that a matter of business had taken him out of London, and she was not to disturb herself if he did not return that day. Rowena frowned as she read it, for this was typical of her brother's behaviour ever since his encounter with Colonel Fury. Physically he had recovered completely from his ordeal, but he had never regained his former frankness and good spirits.

At first, perplexity and irritation were the only emotions inspired in her by his abrupt departure, but on the third morning after it, when no news had reached her and no clue to his whereabouts, she confided her growing uneasiness to Tobias. He frowned over the mystery, and rubbed his lean, shaven jaw.

"Would he have ridden home to Mereworth, Miss Rowena?" he hazarded at length.

"Without baggage or servants, and saying no word to me?" she replied. "That is unlikely."

"I've heard tell Sir Gilroy Mabyn is out of London," Tobias offered next. "Maybe Mr. Peter has gone to join him."

"That is not likely either. I fancy there has been some disagreement between them, for Sir Gilroy visited my brother only once during his illness. I cannot say I am sorry for it."

"Then you should be, mistress," Tobias told her bluntly. "Sir Gilroy be a man you can depend on, and to my mind would be a good friend in any kind of trouble. Aye, you may toss your head, but mark my words! Sir Gilroy's the man who will master *you* in the end."

"Tobias, you go too far!" Rowena's cheeks were flushed and she spoke angrily. "I wish to hear no more of Sir Gilroy. What I do desire is to know what has become of my brother."

"Hoity-toity!" said Tobias, unabashed. "I will see what I can learn, but it had best be done discreetly. If

50

Mr. Peter's off on affairs of his own, he'll not thank us for stirring up a buzz of gossip."

Tobias did his best, but his careful investigations brought no result, and as the days passed, Rowena's fears increased. Mindful of what her servant had said, she showed the world a cheerful face, and when asked where her brother was, said lightly that business had taken him home to Leicestershire, but a deep and growing anxiety was gnawing at her heart. Whenever she went abroad, she found herself looking anxiously for Sir Gilroy Mabyn, for she had begun to think that he might be able to provide some clue to the mystery. The scrap of conversation she had overheard on the day of the quarrel recurred constantly in her memory, echoing as it did Peter's delirious mutterings about seven magpies and Colonel Fury. Undoubtedly Gil Mabyn knew something, and had she seen him she would have humbled herself sufficiently to seek his help, but he seemed to have disappeared as completely as her brother had done.

At last, when more than two weeks had dragged by since Peter's disappearance, and still Sir Gilroy had not returned to London, she felt that she could keep her own counsel no longer. Summoning Tobias, she said without preamble:

"Have you ever heard of the seven magpies? Can you tell me who or what they are?"

Tobias stared. "The seven magpies, Miss Rowena?" he said blankly. "I've not heard tell of it before, but it sounds to me like the name of an inn."

"An inn!" she repeated. "Yes, of course! Why did I not think of that? An inn somewhere on Hounslow Heath!"

Hurriedly she told him of the two occasions when she had heard the Seven Magpies mentioned, and added with conviction: "I have felt all along that Peter's disappearance is in some way connected with what befell him at Colonel Fury's hands. If he believes the man to have some connection with an inn of that name, he may well have gone there in search of him, hoping to avenge the treatment he received."

" 'Tis the kind of hot-headed folly Mr. Peter might attempt," Tobias agreed slowly, "though I would have supposed Sir Gilroy more likely to aid him than to warn him against it. I had best set out for Hounslow as soon as may be."

"We will both set out," Rowena corrected him firmly. "If you think I can endure to wait at home for you to send me news, you are very much mistaken."

From this resolve no amount of argument could shift her, and at last Tobias abandoned the attempt, and went to make preparations for the journey. Mrs. Marriott, who would certainly have protested just as vigorously, and with as little effect, happened to be indisposed that day, and accepted without question Rowena's assertion that she was going to join her brother. By the time she felt well enough to ask for details, her impulsive young kinswoman was already far beyond her reach.

Arriving at Hounslow, they went to one of the better inns, and Tobias, having seen his mistress safely settled there, went out again to see what he could learn in the town. He was gone for some while, and Rowena was in a fret of impatience by the time he returned.

"There *is* an inn called the Seven Magpies, out on the Heath," he said in answer to her anxious question, "but it seems there is little known of it. 'Tis kept by a man named Silas Birley, but he has naught to do with folk hereabouts, and is only seen in the town from time to time when he comes to buy provisions."

"All the more reason to suppose it the place we seek," Rowena said briskly. "You have found out the way to the inn? Then have them fetch the horses, and let us be on our way."

Tobias looked troubled. "Maybe you'd best bide here, Miss Rowena," he suggested. "The inn lies far from the highway, and if there is danger there we shall have no one to call on for aid. I'd not forgive myself if you came to harm."

"The blame would not be yours, since I go with you against your advice," she replied firmly. "Do not try to dissuade me, Tobias, for 'twill be labour lost. Come, let us waste no more time!"

Tobias sighed and went to do her bidding, hoping devoutly that no matter what they discovered at the inn, she would be content to make their visit there a brief one, and that the danger he foresaw would not materialise. His misgivings increased with every mile they rode across the grim waste of the Heath, and when at length the inn came in sight it did nothing to lift his spirits. The day, which had begun bright, had now clouded over, and a chill breeze had sprung up, so that the old, weather-beaten inn crouched beneath a grey sky against its background of twisted trees. As they rode up to the door the only sounds to break the silence were those made by their horses' hooves, the wind in the branches, and the creaking of the faded sign above their heads.

It was Patience who came in answer to Tobias's

shout, and stared wide-eyed to see a fashionably dressed young lady dismounting at her door. The two girls faced each other under the creaking sign-board, the one elegant in a riding-dress of deep green velvet, with gold-laced coat and plumed hat, the other in homespun and coarse linen, her face pale, with a look of haunting sadness in the shadowed eyes. Then Patience, recollecting her duty, dropped a curtsy and ushered the newcomers into the parlour. Rowena sat down on one of the settles and, drawing off her gloves, said with a smile:

"I look to meet my brother here. Has he yet arrived?"

Tobias frowned at this abrupt announcement of their errand, but Patience looked mystified and shook her head.

"No one is here, madam," she replied doubtfully. "Are you certain you have not mistaken the inn?"

"This is the Seven Magpies, is it not? I fancy that my brother has been here before. A tall young man, and, so I am told, somewhat like to me in feature." As she spoke, Rowena took off the wide-brimmed hat which had shadowed her face, and laid it down beside her. "His name is Peter Buckland."

Patience gave a choking gasp and put out a hand blindly to clutch at the table's edge, staring at Rowena as though at a ghost. Her lips moved but no sound emerged, and then she turned and ran from the room and they heard her footsteps receding rapidly along the passage. Rowena looked triumphantly at Tobias.

"You see?" she said in an exultant whisper. "The girl does know something!"

"Have a care, Miss Rowena, in God's name!" Tobias besought her urgently. "Who knows what we may be meddling in?"

"Why, what can it be that I must ask no questions? Have I not the right to search for my brother?"

Tobias made no reply, but shook his head with an air of deep foreboding. As soon as he set eyes on Patience, it had occurred to him that this pretty country girl might well be the reason for his young master's interest in the inn, and even, perhaps, the cause of the dispute between him and Sir Gilroy. Such an explanation had obviously not occurred to Rowena, and Tobias felt that no good purpose would be served by pointing it out to her.

A few minutes passed, and then a heavier footfall was heard approaching, and the innkeeper himself came into the room. Bowing to Rowena, he said apologetically:

"I must crave your pardon for my daughter, madam, but I fear that the gentleman you seek is not known to us."

"Yet I have heard him speak of the Seven Magpies on Hounslow Heath. Perhaps his presence has passed unnoticed among other guests."

Silas Birley shook his head. "This is not a busy house, madam, and all our guests are known to us. Perhaps you have mistaken the name. The magpie is common enough on inn-signs in these parts."

"I do not think so!" Rowena spoke calmly but with finality. "However, we have ridden far and I have not yet supped, so I will take my supper here. Perhaps my brother will arrive while I am at table."

Birley looked as though he would have liked to protest, but made no attempt to do so and withdrew to see about the preparation of a meal. As soon as they were alone, Tobias began to argue, but to all his admonitions Rowena turned a deaf ear. She was certain now that Peter was known at the inn, and nothing could persuade her to abandon the quest.

The meal which was presently set before her was unpretentious but good, and Silas Birley himself helped Tobias to wait upon her. She tried to engage him in conversation, but though he replied with courtesy to all her remarks, she found it impossible to draw him out. His cultured voice and manner, however, were as evident to her as they had been to Peter, and this merely increased her conviction that there were secrets to be discovered.

By the time the meal was over and the cloth removed from the table, the shadows of evening were beginning to fall across the Heath. Rowena, ignoring this fact, said calmly:

"Tobias, I am sure that you are hungry. Pray go with Master Birley, and have your own supper."

"It grows late, Miss Rowena," Tobias replied bluntly. "Time we were on our way."

She glanced towards the window. "Why, so it does, and Hounslow Heath at nightfall does not commend itself to me. We will lie here tonight."

The two men exchanged a startled glance. Birley said courteously: "Madam, I can offer you neither quarters nor attendance befitting a lady of quality."

"More fitting, I am sure, than the open Heath," she replied calmly. "I am not hard to please. As for attendance, your daughter may wait upon me." She caught sight of her servant's disapproving expression and added quickly: "Spare your breath, Tobias, for nothing will persuade me to cross the Heath tonight. Go eat your supper."

Tobias muttered something under his breath and limped out of the room behind the landlord, and Rowena, left alone, took more detailed stock of her surroundings. She crossed to the window and stood for a few minutes studying the desolate prospect it commanded, and then went softly to open the door and peer out. The tap-room opposite was unoccupied and full of shadows, and at the angle of the passage the stairs climbed steeply into darkness. Shivering a little at the brooding silence of the place, she closed the door again and returned to her study of the parlour. The sword above the hearth caught her attention, and she regarded it thoughtfully, putting up her hand to trace the pattern of the cut-steel hilt. Then the sound of the door opening brought her swinging round, as the inn-keeper's daughter slipped into the room. She closed the door and came quickly across to where Rowena stood before the fireplace.

"You must not stay here," she told her in an urgent whisper. "Oh, pray believe that I am trying to help you! Go now, while you may! There is more danger here than you can guess."

Rowena nodded towards the darkening window. "More than lies out yonder, where I might fall prey to any wandering robber?" she said with a smile. "What is your name?"

"Patience, madam, but . . ."

"Patience!" Rowena repeated softly, and once more Peter's feverish murmurings came into her mind. "So it was your name he spoke that day!" With an impulsive gesture she caught the other girl's hands in her own, holding them tightly. "If you wish to help me, tell me what has become of my brother! Is he safe and well? I am nigh crazed with anxiety!"

Patience shook her head staring at her with frightened yet pitying eyes. "I can tell you nothing," she whispered. "You should never have come here! You know not what you risk!"

"Perhaps I can guess!" Rowena released her hands and stepped back; her voice was cold. "If you can tell me nothing of Peter Buckland, here is a name perhaps more familiar. What do you know of Colonel Fury?" Patience uttered a stifled protesting cry, but Rowena went on relentlessly: "Colonel Fury flogged my brother and left him to die, but by a miracle his life was spared. Later, in his pain and fever, Peter spoke your name in the same breath as that of this inn and Colonel Fury. Now he has disappeared, and I think you know what has befallen him. What say you to that, Patience Birley?"

"I say that you are mad!" Patience was staring at her with wide, horrified eyes. "Mad to come here, mad even to whisper such a thing between these walls. Dear God! do you not know the risk you run? I will listen to no more." She went across to the door, but paused with her hand on the latch to look back at the other girl. "I will prepare a room for you, and if you are wise you will lock yourself within it and pray that you may sleep undisturbed. And if your prayers are answered, go from here at first light and give thanks for the rest of your days."

She went out, and Rowena sank down again upon the settle, conscious for the first time of fear, and an uneasy suspicion that her anxiety for her brother had led her into a situation more perilous than she had foreseen. In London, even after Peter's grim experience, Colonel Fury had been no more than a name. Here at this lonely inn, with dusk thickening across the barren waste which stretched for miles on every side, he was fast acquiring a sinister reality.

She was glad when Tobias returned, bringing with him candles to dispel the gloom. He put them down on the table and regarded her grimly.

"This is a sorry plight you have dragged us into, Miss Rowena," he remarked. "Pray God we do not have cause to regret this day's work!"

She looked up eagerly. "Have you learned something?"

"I've been told naught, if that's your meaning, but I've used my eyes and my wits. An inn with no guests, and no servants save an ill-favoured lad in the stables and an old crone half-blind and as deaf as a gate-post. 'I know all who come here,' Master Birley says. Aye, I'll wager he does, and gallows-bait every one, even if Colonel Fury's not among them."

"I believe that he is!" Rowena's voice was subdued. "Patience Birley almost admitted as much when I challenged her." She repeated the conversation she had had with Patience, and it did nothing to ease Tobias's mind.

"He's known here, right enough, and feared also," he said morosely. "We've thrust ourselves into the lion's den, Miss Rowena, and will be lucky if we come off unscathed. Reckon the wench gave you good advice, but what will it profit you if Colonel Fury comes here tonight?"

As though to emphasise his words there came, faint

with distance but drawing swiftly nearer, the sound of approaching hoofbeats. Tobias cursed softly and took a pistol from his pocket, examining it carefully to see that it was ready for instant use. The hoofbeats grew louder—it was a single rider, coming briskly—and Rowena felt her heart quicken with dread. Within the house all was silent, save for the rising wind moaning eerily in the chimney, and suddenly she was in the grip of a cold, sick terror. Any crime could be committed in this desolate spot, and the rest of the world be none the wiser.

The rider reached the inn, and just for an instant she glimpsed him as he passed the window, a fleeting impression, looming huge against the last of the light, of flowing cloak and a broad hat with its plumes rippled by the wind. She rose to her feet in blind panic, remembering what Peter had said of Colonel Fury. "A man bigger than most, and richly dressed." Then a firm footstep sounded, the latch lifted and the door swung open. Framed in the doorway, filling it with his height and breadth, stood Sir Gilroy Mabyn.

For a moment which seemed to hang suspended in time they stared at each other, and she was aware of the smallest, unimportant detail of his appearance, the dust powdering his clothes, and the way the curls of his black periwig had been ruffled and tangled by the wind. Then Tobias said fervently: "Now God be thanked!" and put the pistol back into his pocket.

The homely exclamation seemed to break the spell. Mabyn closed the door behind him and came farther into the room, saying in a tone of mingled astonishment and anger: "Rowena! What in the devil's name are you doing in this place?"

Rowena sat down again abruptly on the settle, for she felt weak and dizzy with a relief she scorned to show. No one, least of all Sir Gilroy himself, must know how thankful she was to see him.

"As to that, sir," she retorted, "I might well ask the same of you."

The words were defiant, but to her dismay the voice she had meant to sound a cool challenge emerged faint and trembling. She cast an appealing glance at Tobias, but he ignored it and, saying that he would see to Sir Gilroy's horse, limped quickly from the room. Rowena, thus deserted, tilted her chin and stared fixedly towards the window.

Sir Gilroy pulled off his gloves, loosed the cloak from his shoulders and dropped it across the table, and tossed his hat carelessly after it. Then he came across to the fireplace, amusement dawning in his eyes as he studied the lady's haughty profile.

"Still so disdainful?" he murmured wickedly. "Yet I am ready to swear that a moment since you were glad to see me."

Indignantly she transferred her gaze to his face. She was still trembling and breathing quickly, and felt uncomfortably certain that this fact had not escaped those observant, teasing eyes, but at least she now had command over her voice.

"I was glad to see you, sir, because I am anxious for news of my brother," she replied, "and if he has been in your company, I take it very much amiss that neither of you saw fit to inform me of it."

"What's this?" Gil spoke sharply, the amusement dying out of his face. "Is Peter not with you?"

Her eyes widened and she shook her head. "Peter, Sir Gilroy, disappeared two weeks ago, and I do not know what has become of him. That is why I came here today, seeking news of him. I did not know where else I might find it."

He frowned at her. "What led you to suppose that you would find it here?"

"Can you not tell me that?"

"I?" He laughed shortly. "I never clapped eyes on this place until tonight, nor have I spoken with Peter since I last visited his house. I have been staying in Warwickshire with my sister."

"And I suppose mere chance brought you here, to an inn hidden away in the midst of Hounslow Heath?" Rowena, too agitated to be still, jumped up and went to stand by the table, staring resentfully at him, "Ah, why do you lie to me? This place is known both to you and to Peter, for I heard you talking of it. You warned him to concern himself no more with the Seven Magpies."

There was a pause before he replied, as though, she thought, he were debating how much, or how little, to admit. Then he said slowly:

"It is true that Peter told me of this place. He believed that Colonel Fury finds refuge here, and he wished me to come with him to confront the rogue, so that he might avenge the humiliation Fury had caused him. I thought the notion foolhardy, and told him so. We quarrelled, and the next day I left London for Warwickshire, but the more I thought on the matter, the more uneasy I became lest Peter venture here alone. I wrote to him, making my peace and bidding him wait until I returned to London and we might talk of it again."

"There was no letter," she relied. "I am sure of it."

"Then it miscarried. I am sorry for that, but the blame is not mine."

"So a letter miscarried!" Rowena's voice was scornful. "And Sir Gilroy Mabyn puts on the mantle of wise and prudent counsellor, and seeks to curb the recklessness of his friend. That is indeed the devil rebuking sin!"

"It is the truth," he said quietly.

She turned abruptly away and stood staring at the candle-flames, shaken in spite of herself. Extravagant denials would have left her unmoved, but those few simple words carried a conviction which could not be denied; and she wanted to believe him. She was startled to discover how much she wanted it.

"So you know nothing of Peter's whereabouts?" she said slowly.

"Nothing, on my life! Until now I believed him to be at home in London, but one thing I promise you. If he *has* been here, I will discover it, and also where he is now to be found."

The words reminded Rowena of her own fruitless quest, and at the same time pointed out to her a flaw in Sir Gilroy's explanation. Hoping desperately that she was mistaken, she said:

"If you knew nothing of Peter's disappearance, sir, and were, in fact, expecting to meet him in London, what brings you to the Seven Magpies tonight?"

This time he did not reply, and when, with a sinking heart, she turned to look at him, she surprised in his face an expression similar to that which he had worn when he strode out of her brother's room after their quarrel.

"Nothing which has anything to do with Peter," he said at last. "That is all I can tell you."

"Peter told you of this place, and yet your first visit here in no ways concerns him? You ask me to believe that?"

"I ask you to accept my word that it is so."

"How can I, when you will not tell me what really brings you here?" She spoke pleadingly, but his expression did not soften, and her earlier suspicions returned in full force. "You are hiding something from me! You *do* know what has become of Peter!"

"I know nothing, but whatever has happened, you may safely leave me to discover it. In the morning you must return to London. I will bring word to you there as soon as may be."

"No, I will not! The people here know something of my brother, and I will not go until I have discovered what it is. You cannot persuade me, and you have not the right to command."

He moved away from the fireplace and came to stand before her, looking down into her face. In his own dark countenance the grim expression still lingered, but now there was a hint of mocking laughter in his eyes.

"You are wilful and headstrong and permitted to have too much your own way," he said softly, "but you cannot browbeat *me,* my sweet termagant, nor will I allow you to court danger of the sort which lurks here. Mistrust me if you must, but you may be glad of the

64

chance which brought me so hard upon your foolish heels." She started to protest, but his hand shot out to grip her arm and he lifted his head to listen. "Someone comes," he said after a moment, "and if 'tis Colonel Fury, or even one of his followers, you had best accept my protection with what grace you may."

Before she could reply, Tobias came hurrying into the room and looked anxiously at Sir Gilroy.

"There's a rider approaching, sir," he announced, "and from the looks of the landlord and his daughter, 'tis one who is expected if not welcome."

Gil nodded, and by an insistent pressure on Rowena's arm drew her towards the nearest settle and obliged her to sit down. As she obeyed, her fears returned and it was with difficulty that she resisted a childish impulse to clutch at his hand as it was withdrawn. As though aware of it, he glanced down at her with a swift, reassuring smile, and remained standing beside her, one hand resting on the back of the settle.

They heard the rider reach the inn and dismount, and a moment or two later the door of the parlour was flung abruptly open. From the threshold a tall man in a wine-red coat, his swarthy face shadowed by a plumed hat, stared menacingly upon them, one hand gripping the hilt of his sword. Sir Gilroy was the first to break the silence.

"Colonel Fury, I believe?" he said with mocking courtesy. "My dear sir, we have awaited your coming most eagerly!"

The highwayman, who had been staring at him with narrowed eyes, took a pace forward and kicked the door shut behind him. The surprise which for an instant had flickered across his face was gone, leaving behind it a sardonic amusement made sinister by the menace of his glance.

"There is only one man who would dare to take that tone with me," he said in a harsh, arrogant voice. "You always did possess the devil's own insolence, Gil Mabyn!"

4

Colonel Fury

He did not seem to expect a reply, but looked curiously from Sir Gilroy to Rowena, his dark glance lingering upon her with bold admiration. She was scarcely aware of his regard, for her mind was still reeling from the shock of discovering that Colonel Fury, the brutal robber who had flogged Peter and left him to die, was apparently upon terms of familiarity with Sir Gilroy Mabyn. It made the reason for Gil's own presence at the inn seem hideously clear.

"I do not think," Colonel Fury remarked, "that I am acquainted with the lady."

"Allow me to present you!" Gil's voice was ironic. "My dear, permit me to make known to you Colonel Fury, England's most notorious highwayman. Colonel, Miss Rowena Buckland."

He spoke the name with some deliberation, but apparently it conveyed nothing to the highwayman. He swept off his hat and bowed with a courtier's grace.

"Madam, your servant. It is not often that we are favoured here with so charming a guest."

She inclined her head in acknowledgment and

murmured some response, fighting against a sense of unreality. He might have been any gentleman of the Court, uttering elaborate compliments while his eyes appraised her with bold approval, and it was hard to remember that he was guilty of countless robberies and more than one cold-blooded murder, as well as the kind of wanton brutality of which Peter had been a victim. His manner made her fears seem absurd, and for an instant she was tempted to ask him outright if he knew what had become of her brother, but as though Gil had guessed her intention and meant to thwart it, he reached out to take her hand in a hard, warning grip, saying smoothly:

"Very likely you are not, and I regret that you will not have the opportunity of enjoying Miss Buckland's company. She was about to retire." His grasp on her hand compelled Rowena to rise, and without knowing quite how it was accomplished she found herself somehow at the door, with Gil still holding her by the hand. In the background Colonel Fury was bowing again, and hiding whatever chagrin he might feel behind a mask of arrogant courtesy.

"You may sleep soundly, Rowena. There is naught to fret you," Gil said with quiet meaning, and raised her hand to his lips before releasing it. "Tobias, attend your mistress."

Tobias, with a look of grim approval, ushered Rowena firmly out of the parlour, and as the door closed behind them Gil turned to confront Colonel Fury. The highwayman regarded him with a scowl.

"High-handed as ever, are you not?" he said threateningly. "You would do well to remember that you are not now lording it among subservient lackeys in your ancestral home. Here, it is I who call the tune."

"Not where Miss Buckland is concerned," Gil corrected him, "so let us understand each other on that score at the outset. She is the lady whom I intend to make my wife, and if ever you cause her the least harm or distress, then as God sees me, Kennet, I will kill you!"

He spoke quietly, almost pleasantly, but with an emphasis which showed that this was no idle threat. Fury's glance silently acknowledged it, but he said with no lessening of his arrogant manner:

"So that is the future Lady Mabyn! Could you find no more idyllic surroundings than these in which to pursue your wooing?" He did not wait for a reply, but strode across to fling open the door and loose a shout for the innkeeper. "Ho there, Silas Birley! Bestir yourself, and bring us wine!" Turning back to Gil, he added mockingly: "I take it that you will drink with me?"

"I will drink with you," Gil agreed coolly, "and then, if you please, we will talk of the matter which brings me here."

"We'll talk of something else first," Fury said curtly, coming back into the room. "How did you know where to find me?"

Gil did not reply at once, but paused to settle himself comfortably in the elbow-chair at the head of the table, leaving his companion no choice but to stand, or to sit upon bench or settle. A flicker of anger lit the highwayman's dark eyes for an instant at Mabyn's calm assumption of the place of honour, but he made no remark, and merely moved to take up a position in front of the fireplace, his back to the gaping hearth.

"From one of your victims," Gil said at length. "You should have guessed that your arrogant refusal to disguise yourself would sooner or later lead to your being recognised."

Fury frowned. "I'll swear I have held up no one who could betray me."

"You mean that you have let no one who recognised you live to tell of it," Gil retorted contemptuously. "To see your face is a death-warrant for any who chance to know it! No, the man who led me to you is not acquainted with you. I had suspected the truth for some time, for I felt certain that you had returned to the road, and Colonel Fury's exploits accorded so well with what I know of your character. Then you were described to me very accurately by one who had good cause to remember your face, and suspicion became certainty."

He broke off as Silas Birley came in bearing wine and glasses, and while he set them on the table and poured the wine, the other two men remained silent. The innkeeper looked curiously at Gil, but apparently Tobias had informed him of Mabyn's identity, for before leaving the parlour he inquired courteously whether Sir Gilroy desired to bespeak a room for the night. Gil nodded.

"If you please. I wait to escort Miss Buckland back to London in the morning. Colonel Fury, I am sure, will give us safe-conduct."

The last words were uttered with a sardonic glance at the highwayman, who laughed shortly.

"I'll think on't," he said with a sneer. "Much depends upon how well we agree tonight." He waited until Birley had left the room and then added brusquely:

"So you discovered that I was Colonel Fury. What is that to you?"

Gil shrugged and picked up his glass of wine. "Little enough, as long as Colonel Fury remains at liberty! You will agree it would be a very different matter if he were captured and brought to trial." He lifted the glass in salutation. "Let us drink to our good agreement."

"As you will!" Fury lifted his own glass, and drank. "You have not yet told me the means by which you learned that this inn is my hiding-place."

"We will come to that directly. First to the purpose which brings me here." He set down the glass and leaned forward. "Five thousand pounds in gold, Kennet, if you will take yourself out of England for good."

Fury stared at him in silence for a moment with narrowed eyes, and then returned to contemplation of the wine remaining in his glass. He said reflectively:

"Five thousand pounds! A handsome offer, Gil! You have it with you?"

"Oh, to be sure!" Gil flung himself back in his chair, his eyes bright with mockery beneath their black brows. "I carry it about me, so that you may cut my throat with some profit to yourself! What manner of fool do you think I am? You receive the gold when you step ashore in France, and not before."

With some deliberation Colonel Fury emptied his glass and came to the table to refill it. With it in his hand, he stood looking down at Mabyn, his swarthy face wearing an expression of cruel contempt.

"Why should I go into exile merely to please you?" he asked. "This life suits me very well, and is profitable into the bargain. Five thousand pounds would not sustain me for a twelvemonth."

"Remain in England, and you may not live another twelvemonth. No man can provoke the kind of hatred you do, and not be betrayed in the end. Better France and five thousand pounds than Tyburn's triple tree!"

"To the devil with that!" Fury moved to the settle and sat down, one foot on the seat and his elbow resting on his bent knee. "I have had too close an acquaintance with death these five-and-twenty years to fear it unduly now, and if I must needs quit this world by way of Tyburn Fair, then, by God, I'll die as I have lived, and give the mob good reason to make holiday!" He tossed off the wine and looked across at Mabyn with a grin. "What if I decline the offer? I know full well that *you* will never give me up to the Law!"

"There *is* another way," Gil told him quietly, and laid his hand significantly on the hilt of his sword.

Fury laughed. "You think you *could* rid yourself of me thus?"

"It is possible! Oh, I know you are a great swordsman, but I am no novice myself, and much of the art I learned from you! Also, I am the younger by close upon twenty years."

For a few moments Fury appeared to consider this. Then he nodded.

"I will own it is possible. It would suit you very well, would it not, to kill me thus, here and now, and no one any the wiser?"

"Excellently well! It would save a deal of trouble *and* five thousand pounds. Shall we summon Tobias and the innkeeper, and cross swords now, or do you prefer to wait for daylight?"

"It is possible," the highwayman repeated, as though Gil had not spoken, "but it is also possible that I might kill you. I know you would not shrink from risking that—not, that is, upon your own account." He was watching the younger man closely, and laughed softly to see the sudden angry dismay in his eyes. "But that would leave the charming lady above-stairs with no protector save a crippled serving-man. By Heaven, Gil Mabyn! What imp of folly possessed you to bring her with you upon such an errand?"

Sir Gilroy did not reply at once. For a few moments he had forgotten that Rowena was at the inn, that she had plunged headlong into a peril the magnitude of which she had not paused to contemplate. When at last he did speak again, it seemed at first as though his words had no connection with the highwayman's remark, and Fury scowled with angry perplexity at their apparent irrelevancy.

"A while since you asked me how I discovered this bolt-hole of yours, and now I will tell you. I was told of it by the same man who described you to me—Peter Buckland." He moved his head in a gesture indicating the rooms above, and added in explanation: "Her brother."

Fury's frown deepened. "I know no Peter Buckland!"

"No? But you remember, no doubt, the young man whom you flogged and would have murdered on the Heath not long ago?"

Colonel Fury had been twisting his empty glass idly between his fingers, but for an instant it was still while he directed a piercing glance at Gil. Then he shrugged, and fell to toying with the glass again.

"I remember! An insolent cub who was rash enough to take a high tone with me. I left him to ponder the folly of his conduct, and when I returned he had made his escape. Had I known then that he was brother to *your* chosen bride, I would have seen to it that escape was impossible."

"You intended it to be impossible in any event!" Gil's voice was contemptuous. "Peter had stumbled upon this place, and because the doxy you keep here knew a moment's pity and sent him on his way, you were obliged to hunt him down. Then instead of killing him outright you flogged him half to death, and left him to suffer until it suited you to return and finish your murderous work. Why, Kennet? Was it because your wench looked kindly upon him, and so reminded you that you begin to grow old? Was jealousy the spur which goaded you to torture him?"

"Damnation!" Fury leapt to his feet, casting the glass from him to shatter into fragments on the hearth. In two strides he was standing beside Gil's chair, towering over him, his dark face congested with anger. "I am still young enough to deal with that puppy, and a dozen like him. Aye, and to send *you* before me into hell, Gil Mabyn!"

"As you have now sent Peter Buckland?" The question, softly spoken, thrust itself into Fury's tirade, but if Gil hoped that the highwayman's rage would betray him, the hope was vain. Only the barest change of expression flickered for an instant in the dark eyes. Fury said bitterly:

"As I *should* have sent him, but he escaped to betray my secret, to you of all men, and no doubt to his sister also." He paused, and slowly the anger faded from his face and a cruel smile dawned about his mouth. "And you were mad enough to bring her here," he added softly, "to the one place where I am master! Before God, I never supposed you could be so great a fool!"

"I did not bring her," Gil said shortly. "She heard her brother speak of this place to me, and now that he has disappeared, she seeks news of him here." He thrust back the chair and rose abruptly to his feet. "I seek it also, Kennet, so do not lie to me! What has become of Peter Buckland?"

For a few seconds they confronted each other in silence, two big, dark men who, each knowing the other to be dangerous, scorned to disguise their mutual contempt and dislike. Then Fury laughed shortly and turned away.

"Seek, and be damned to you!" he said coldly. "I know not where he is."

Gil's lips tightened, and for a moment he seemed tempted to cast caution aside and resort to violence. His hand went to his sword and gripped hard on the hilt, and Fury, observing it, laughed again.

"How it would please you to run me through," he sneered, "and how galling to your pride that you dare not attempt it, lest you leave unguarded the prize you rode hot-foot from London to protect."

Instead of provoking Gil to greater anger, the taunt seemed somehow to help him to self-control. He let go the sword and turned instead to fill his glass again.

"I can be patient," he said coolly. "As for my following Miss Buckland from London, you are quite mistaken. I have come straight from Warwickshire."

"The devil you have!" There was a mordant amusement now in Fury's harsh voice. "So the bargain you seek to strike is not upon your own behalf alone. You are merely the appointed emissary."

"That need not concern you. The offer stands—five thousand pounds if you agree to leave England and trouble us no more—and to my mind 'tis a deal more than you deserve. A foot or so of steel would serve the same purpose, and with more certainty."

" 'Tis true the only certainty in life is death," the highwayman agreed calmly, "and even if I accept your bargain, you will never be sure that I shall not return. So much for that! What if I refuse?"

Gil shrugged. "Then no doubt in due course you will take the ride to Tyburn, and others beside yourself will suffer. Remember, we can no more protect you than we can, for our own sake, give you up to the Law. If you are taken alive, you will hang!"

"The same might be said of any man who works the bridle-lay! However, the offer you make will bear thinking on! I can tarry here no longer, for I have business to attend to, but I will return in the morning. You shall have your answer then."

"Then be not too tardy," Gil replied curtly. "It is my intention to leave this place betimes. The sooner Miss Buckland is safely back in London, the easier my mind will be."

"So will not mine!" Fury retorted. "*You* I can depend upon not to inform against me, but what of her? I've no mind to be betrayed by the babbling of a silly wench who fancies she has a grudge against me."

Gil leaned against the table's edge and lifted his glass, studying the colour of the wine as the light glowed through it.

"You may safely leave Miss Buckland to me," he

said quietly. " 'Twill be against my interests if you are brought to trial, and you have my word that she will be given no opportunity to lay information against you. Does that content you?"

For a moment the highwayman regarded him in silence and with some suspicion. Then Sir Gilroy's gaze lifted from the glass of wine to meet his, the brilliant, blue-green eyes cool and challenging. Colonel Fury laughed.

"It contents me," he replied, "for I've no doubt you know well enough how to bend a woman to your will. So be it, then!" He turned to pick up the gloves he had dropped on to the table, strode across to the door and paused there to look back at Gil. "Your offer tempts me, I'll not deny, but I've no mind to accept it without due thought. All depends upon where I may find the greatest profit."

He went out and along the stone-flagged passage, past the foot of the stairs and so to the kitchen beyond. The old woman was dozing in the chimney corner, but Patience and her father stood by the big table in the middle of the room, talking in low voices. They broke off abruptly as he entered, and he acknowledged the fact with a sneer.

"Aye, curb your tongues," he said unpleasantly, "and see to it that you are equally discreet with your new guests yonder. What questions have they asked you?"

"The young lady seeks news of her brother, but we deny all knowledge of him," Birley replied. "The gentleman has asked no questions of us yet, for he arrived here only a short while before you yourself rode up."

"He *will* question you, I'll warrant, and I give you fair warning. Sir Gilroy Mabyn is an ill man to trifle with, and one not easy to deceive." He looked at Patience, the sneer deepening about his lips as she shrank away from him. "Had you turned to such as he, my dear, instead of to the other young spark, you might perhaps have been rid of me. But spare your pains now! He is enamoured of the wilful piece above-stairs."

He pulled her roughly towards him and bent to kiss her, but she set both hands against his chest and thrust him away. In astonishment he let her go, and his lip thinned to an ugly line.

"You grow shrewish, my girl!" he said in a menacing voice. "It does not please me. Take heed lest I find it needful to read you another lesson in obedience."

Patience, overcome by her own temerity, cowered back against the table, staring at him in panic-stricken entreaty. He looked at her contemptuously and then turned away, saying over his shoulder:

"I shall return in the morning, for I have business with Sir Gilroy. Have a care what you say meanwhile, lest you thrust your own necks into a noose as well as mine."

He went out and into the stable, where the lad Thomas was idling, and signed to him to saddle his horse. While this was being done, Colonel Fury occupied himself by examining the three other mounts. Thomas, glancing at him, at length ventured a remark:

"Good beasts, Colonel, all three of 'em. Especially the roan."

The highwayman nodded, running his hand down the neck of Sir Gilroy's powerful roan gelding. "The devil they are, Thomas, though the mare is too dainty for my taste. A lady's mount!" He followed as Thomas led the saddled horse from its stall out into the yard, and there took the bridle from the lad's hand. "Three excellent beasts," he added thoughtfully. "Thomas, you know what to do."

Without waiting for a reply, he mounted and rode off into the silent emptiness of the Heath. The moon peered fitfully between wind-driven clouds, and in its uncertain light the great waste of sand and scrub lay like a dead world. A man might lose his way there a dozen times in an hour, but to Colonel Fury it was his own domain, and he rode without hesitation across its trackless expanse.

Once a group of sheep, startled by his approach, broke from the shelter of a thicket to scatter before him with protesting bleats, but he met no other sign of life until he reached a little hollow not far from the Bath road. Bushes grew thickly there, a mass of black shadow filling the hollow from end to end, but when the Colonel drew rein on the sloping ground above and whistled a snatch of melody, an answer came echoing up to him and there was movement amid the shadows. After a moment the shape of a horse and rider grew out of the darkness and came to join him in the dim radiance of the moon.

"The hour be long past, Colonel," the newcomer greeted him hoarsely. "I'd begun to fear some mischance!"

"I was delayed," Fury replied briefly, "and now I have work of another sort for you to do. It will mean a long ride, and a hard one, but you shall be well rewarded."

79

The other man pushed back his hat to scratch his head, and the faint moonlight revealed a long cadaverous face with a broken nose. He appeared to accept the change of plan philosophically.

"You be a man o' your word, Colonel Fury, sir," he remarked, "and if there's gold at the end of it, Jed Hollett's not the one to shrink from a hard ride. Ye can trust me to do your bidding."

"I can trust you as long as I pay you well," Fury retorted cynically, "but remember! I reward everyone according to his deserts, enemies as well as friends. Now harken to me! I desire you to go, with all possible speed, to Long Padworth in Warwickshire, and there to make inquiry for Sir Marley Falmer, who is the squire of those parts."

"Sir Marley Falmer o' Long Padworth in Warwickshire," Hollett repeated stolidly. "What d'ye wish to know of him, Colonel?"

"I desire to know how the world uses him at this present time. What members of his family dwell with him, and what is the state of his health. Take care not to draw attention upon yourself. You should be able to learn all that is needful from gossip at the village inn or local market-place." He pulled a purse from his pocket and held it out. "Here's for your needs on the journey. There will be as much again for you when you return, but I look to see you at the Seven Magpies three nights hence."

"I'll be there, Colonel!" Hollett took the purse and stowed it away. Then, with a gesture of farewell, he set spur to his horse and rode off towards the north.

For a minute or two Colonel Fury remained on the rim of the hollow, listening to the hoofbeats fading away into the distance. He was smiling to himself with some satisfaction.

"So, Gil Mabyn," he said softly, "we shall see whether your offer is as generous as it seems, or whether you make it to cheat me of greater profit!"

The sound of Jed Hollett's going had faded into the silence of the windswept Heath. Colonel Fury touched his horse with the spur, and rode briskly towards the Bath road.

5

"Trust Me or No—!"

In her bedchamber at the Seven Magpies, Rowena lay
sleepless, torn by conflicting emotions. Outside her
window, the inn-sign shook to and fro in the wind, its
rusty ironwork screeching, and somewhere not far off
an owl called repeatedly, but upon neither of these
melancholy sounds could she blame her wakefulness.
Her body was weary, but her thoughts spun ceaselessly
and would not be still.

She had scarcely known whether to be glad or sorry
when Sir Gilroy ushered her so firmly out of Colonel
Fury's presence, but she had been aware of the necessity of knowing what passed between the two men after
her departure. Tobias, however, with an obtuseness
which exasperated her almost beyond endurance, had
not paused to consult her wishes, but immediately summoned Patience Birley to bring candles and attend
Miss Buckland to bed. Precious time had been wasted
in getting rid of the girl, and in persuading Tobias, who
had stationed himself outside her door, that it was es-
sential to learn what bond existed between Sir Gilroy
Mabyn and the notorious highwayman. When finally he

had been convinced, he took it for granted that he should be the one to eavesdrop upon them, and protested vigorously at Rowena's intention of doing so herself. Only when she pointed out that his lame leg would make it impossible for him to retreat quickly should the need arise did he allow her to have her way.

At last, after a delay which drove her almost to distraction, she crept downstairs in stockinged feet, with her trailing skirts caught up in one hand, and arrived outside the parlour door just in time to hear Sir Gilroy repeat his offer of five thousand pounds, adding his personal opinion that a foot or so of steel would meet the case equally well. Rigid with shock, shaken by incredulous dismay, she had listened appalled to a conversation which seemed to indicate a shameful secret shared by Gil Mabyn and Fury. When movement within the room warned her that the highwayman was about to leave, she fled noiselessly to the stairs, and from their sheltering darkness watched him go past towards the rear of the house. Then she had returned to the anxious Tobias, and, brushing aside his questions, locked herself at once in her room.

In a daze, scarcely aware of what she was doing, she removed her outer garments and lay down upon the bed, drawing the covers up to her chin but unable to check a shivering which was caused by no physical cold. A sick dismay engulfed her. She seemed no nearer to solving the mystery of Peter's disappearance, but at that hour, and in those surroundings, the wildest theories seemed feasible. She remembered that, if Peter were to die, his fortune would pass to her and thence to the man she married. Suppose Gil Mabyn, knowing this, had conspired with Colonel Fury . . . ? Rowena moved restlessly, telling herself that she was mad even to think of it. Sir Gilroy was a rich man, richer than Peter ever had been or would be. Yet, whispered a small, treacherous voice in her thoughts, he was a notorious gambler and as wildly extravagant as any man at Court. It might be that his fortune stood in need of mending. If that were so, then by her folly she had delivered herself completely into his hands.

After what seemed a very long time she heard a footfall on the stairs, and then Sir Gilroy's voice speaking quietly to Tobias, who apparently still kept watch outside her door. She could not make out the words, but after a little a door opened and closed nearby, and then Tobias's uneven footsteps went softly away. She listened to them unbelievingly, and, though scarcely knowing what she feared, lay with tense muscles and pounding heart while the wind moaned round the eaves of the old inn and the signboard creaked and swayed outside the window.

No other sound disturbed the stillness, and after a while she gradually relaxed, but it was a long time before she slept. Even when sleep came at last, it was threaded with uneasy dreams in which the figures of Gil Mabyn and Colonel Fury merged into one, and she fought against a terror and a misery too great to be borne.

It was broad daylight when she awoke, heavy-eyed and unrefreshed, and conscious of thankful surprise that the night had been undisturbed by anything but her own fears. A soft scratching at the door caused her to sit upright in alarm, but reassurance came with Patience Birley's voice asking if Miss Buckland required her attendance. She rose and admitted the girl, hoping to question her again, with more success, concerning the visit which she felt sure Peter must have paid to the inn, but Patience was no more communicative than she had been the previous day. She was sorry, but she did not know the gentleman.

Rowena, seated on a stool before an inadequate mirror, was tying the lace cravat beneath her chin, but she paused to look searchingly at Patience. The blue eyes gazed back at her, dark with entreaty, and she saw the betraying quiver of the delicate lips.

"I think you are lying, Patience Birley," she said quietly, "but I do not know why. If 'tis Colonel Fury you fear, I swear he shall never know what you may tell me. All I desire is to be assured of my brother's well-being, and once I am certain that all *is* well with him, I will go back to London."

Patience shook her head. "You should have gone last night, before *he* found you here," she said in a low voice. "Escape from this place is not so easy that the chance of it may be lightly cast aside."

"I shall leave when I choose," Rowena retorted boldly, hiding a sudden uneasiness beneath a confident manner. She regarded Patience with a frown. "Are you trying to tell me that my brother found himself in a trap here of Colonel Fury's setting?"

"I am trying to tell you nothing! I can tell you nothing!" Patience repeated in a breaking voice. "In pity's name, ask me no more! Be patient, and trust in God, and one day, perhaps, you may understand and forgive!"

She broke off, sobbing wildly, and buried her face in her hands. Rowena jumped up and in a sudden rush of self-reproach put her arms about her.

"Do not weep, child! I'll question you no more. Before Heaven, they must have treated you vilely to make you fear them so!"

Patience dried her eyes with her apron and looked up at Rowena, for the other girl was the taller by several inches. "Ah, you are kind!" she whispered. "As kind and generous as . . ." she broke off, pressing a fold of the apron against her lips. "I pray to God that you will come to no harm! Listen to me, Miss Buckland! When Colonel Fury returns, speak him fair, however discourteous he may seem. Do not anger him, as you value your life, or even Sir Gilroy may not be able to protect you."

"So!" Rowena let her go and moved away, feeling a sudden coldness about her heart. "You know Sir Gilroy, then? He has been here before?"

"No, not until last night. Your servant, Master Thorne, told us of him. He says he is a very gallant gentleman."

"A gallant gentleman who consorts with highwaymen," Rowena said bitterly. "Tobias must be besotted if he trusts him still. Oh, you may go, Patience, you may go! I will remember your warning, and I thank you for it."

Patience hesitated, watching her with troubled, tear-filled eyes, and then she turned and went quietly out of the room. Rowena finished dressing very slowly, aware of a reluctance to leave the apparent sanctuary of her room and confront Sir Gilroy again. Whatever happened, the meeting must be fraught with embarrassment.

When at length she entered the parlour, he was already there, standing beside the table upon which a simple meal was spread. He greeted her with his usual easy courtesy, as though they had met by chance upon a journey and no such person as Colonel Fury existed, and this filled her with irrational vexation. She should have known, she thought irritably, that Gilroy Mabyn would allow nothing to put him out of countenance.

She returned his greeting coldly, determined not to be outdone in civility, but when he would have led her to table, she shook her head and said frigidly that it was not her custom to take breakfast.

" 'Tis a custom which should be broken when a journey lies ahead," he replied calmly. "I've no mind to have you fainting from hunger before we are half way across the Heath."

Rowena eyed him with dislike. "I informed you yesterday, sir, that I have no intention of leaving the inn until I am told what has become of my brother. And when I do leave, Tobias is the only escort I shall need."

"Tobias, being a man of sound common sense, may not agree with you. Besides, what do you suppose you will achieve by remaining? Whatever has become of Peter, you will serve no good purpose by placing yourself in danger, so let us have an end of these tantrums." He paused, regarding her with some amusement, and put out a compelling hand. "Will you come to table, madam?"

For a few seconds she continued to face him defiantly, then, ignoring the outstretched hand, moved to seat herself in the chair at the table's head. She was not sure why she should do so. She had had no intention of sitting down to breakfast with Sir Gilroy Mabyn, for the situation was tinged with an intimacy which she found disquieting, but it seemed more dignified to agree than to stand bickering over so trivial a matter. So she took her place in disdainful silence, and vented her annoyance upon Tobias when, coming in to wait upon them, he was rash enough to express the hope that she had slept well.

"Sleep?" she repeated indignantly. "How could any woman sleep in this den of thieves, where she might be ravished or murdered at any moment?"

"You were in no danger, Miss Rowena," Tobias replied soothingly. "I stayed outside your door until I was certain Colonel Fury had left the inn, and only went to my own rest when I knew that Sir Gilroy was within call."

Rowena made no reply to this, but lifted her brows in an eloquent expression of incredulous disdain. Gil chuckled.

"Miss Buckland clearly numbers me among those who threaten her safety," he murmured, "but at least acquit me, madam, of having any desire to murder you."

Rowena gasped, and choked. Recovering, she said with as much dignity as scarlet cheeks would allow: "Your own conduct, sir, is to blame if I am reluctant to trust you. I might more readily accept your protection if you were upon less intimate terms with Colonel Fury."

There was a moment's silence, and then he said lightly: "It is not always wise, madam, to judge a man by the company he keeps. Necessity makes strange bedfellows."

Rowena put down her knife and thrust her plate away, finding that her appetite had suddenly deserted her. All the dark suspicions of the night returned to plague her, recalled and seemingly confirmed by the careless words. Necessity bound him to Colonel Fury, and he was waiting now to know whether the highwayman would accept the bargain he had proposed.

Gil regarded her for a moment or two longer, a faint frown in his eyes, but made no comment. In leisurely fashion he finished his meal, and then signed to Tobias to leave them. Rowena, who had been staring before her, lost in thought, looked up with a start as the door closed and made as though to follow him, but Gil stretched out his hand to grasp her wrist.

"I can only ask you to trust me," he said quietly. "I cannot tell you what brings me here, what business I have with Colonel Fury."

"There is no need to tell me," she replied fiercely. "You are here to try to bribe him to leave England, because you fear what may come to light if he is brought to trial. You wait now for him to return with his answer."

Gil did not move, still leaning forward across the corner of the table with his hand on her wrist, but the gentle clasp had become a vice-like grip, and his eyes were narrowed now, brilliant and jewel-hard.

"So you know that, do you?" he said softly. "How much did you hear besides?"

"Enough to know that *I* am to be given no chance to betray you, or your outlaw comrade! That you know how to bend me to your will! And you ask me to trust you!"

He let her go, and she thrust back the chair and jumped to her feet, rubbing her wrist where his fingers had left a red mark.

"Did Peter stumble upon your secret, too?" she asked with angry contempt. "Did you seek to bend him also, and beak him when he would not bend?" A sob quivered in her voice. "Ah, dear God! where is he? What have you done to him?"

Gil got up and came round the table to stand beside her, but he did not touch her again. He said in a low voice:

"I do not know what has become of Peter, but if Fury knows, then for good or ill I will discover it. For the rest, I *had* to stand surety for your silence, or your life would not be worth a moment's purchase. He will kill without mercy to safeguard himself."

Abruptly she swung round, turning her back upon him, but was still acutely aware of him standing so close beside her. She was a tall girl, but Sir Gilroy towered over her, making her feel small and helpless, in mind as well as in body. She did not know what to believe. Reason and logic warned her to distrust him, but a deeper instinct urged her another way.

"Trust me or no, I love you," he said quietly. "Rowena..."

The door was flung open and Tobias came back into the room, hurriedly, with no apology for the intrusion or even an awareness of the need for one. "A sorry plight we are in now, Sir Gilroy," he said grimly. "Our horses have gone!"

Gil, who had turned angrily towards him as he entered, checked whatever rebuke he had been about to utter and instead said curtly: "You are certain of it?"

"Certain as death, sir! I went to look to them and found the stable empty, and the lad who was supposed to tend 'em gone as well. Master Birley pretends to know nothing of it, and I can't shift him from that, for all I know he's lying."

"You mean that our horses have been stolen from out of the very stable?" Rowena exclaimed incredulously. "Oh, it is outrageous!"

" 'Tis worse than that, my dear," Gil told her in a hard voice. "It means that we are as good as prisoners, stranded here until Colonel Fury sees fit to afford us the means to leave."

"Any chance of crossing the Heath on foot, sir?" Tobias queried.

Gil shook his head. "You or I might attempt it, but not Miss Buckland, and even we would run the risk of being seen and ridden down by Fury's men. He means us to remain here. That much is certain, and for the present we have no choice but to abide by his wishes."

Rowena stared at him with deepening suspicion, the desire to believe in him still strong within her, but overwhelmed now by an even stronger tide of doubt.

"You take the matter vary calmly, sir," she said challengingly, "but perhaps it is not as great a shock to you as it is to me."

He glanced sharply at her. "What mean you by that?"

"I mean, Sir Gilroy, that it is unlike you to yield so tamely to the dictates of a man such as Colonel Fury unless it accords with your own plans to do so. That perhaps it suits your purpose to keep us here."

He looked down at her with a touch of irony. "It was not I, madam, who a few minutes since was asserting an unshakable determination to remain in this place. *My* intention, you may recall, was to return you to London with all possible speed."

Rowena tossed her head. Her accusation had been prompted more by anger and dismay than by any reasoned thought, but she resented the fact that he had pointed out the absurdity of it. Always he seemed to put her in the wrong.

"To stay because I wish to, sir, is one thing," she retorted. "To stay because I must is quite another."

"An unanswerable piece of feminine logic," he commented, "and far beyond the comprehension of any mere man. But from choice or necessity, sweetheart, stay you must, so do your best to grow reconciled to that fact." To Tobias he added: "I believe it will be wise to make no great noise over the loss of the horses. I cannot yet perceive what reason Fury has for wishing to keep us here, but until we do discover it, let us accept the situation with as good a grace as we may."

Tobias, who in spite of everything appeared to be still quite ready to put complete trust in Sir Gilroy, agreed to this and went off again to the kitchen. Gil turned back to Rowena, who still stood rigidly by the table. She stared resentfully at him.

"For how long, sir, do you suppose your highwayman friend proposes to keep us imprisoned here?" she asked bitterly. "And how are we to occupy ourselves in this Godforsaken spot?"

Laughter leapt into his eyes again. He seemed to have abandoned the serious mood which had preceded Tobias's news, and the quiet sincerity which had then sounded in his voice might never have been.

"I fancy we might profitably employ the time in becoming better acquainted," he suggested. "Hitherto you have been so studious in avoiding my company, and so ready to lend ear to any tale told to my discredit, that it is small wonder you distrust me now."

Her brows lifted. "Do you tell me, sir, that the tales I have heard are false?"

"Devil a one," he replied cheerfully, "but no man is as black as he is painted, and since we are to be married . . ."

"We are not!" she broke in sharply. "I know that my brother desires the match, but you assume too much, Sir Gilroy, if you imagine that I am agreeable to it. Let us understand each other upon that. I will not marry you!"

Leaning his folded arms on the back of the big chair, he regarded her with amused curiosity. "You are emphatic, madam! May I ask why?"

"You need to ask?" Rowena's voice was scornful. "So be it, then! When I marry, sir, it will not be a dissolute libertine, an idle frequenter of taverns and playhouses. I am not sufficiently fashionable to love the loose ways of the Court, nor am I prepared to share my husband with every bold wench of Whitehall and Drury Lane." She paused, eyeing him defiantly. "Are you answered?"

"Completely, madam!" He stood erect again and moved towards her and she forced herself to stand her ground, even when he took her lightly by the shoulders. "And you believe me to be just such a scoundrel, a rake-hell to whom no woman's honour is sacred?"

Held thus before him, scorning to struggle or turn away, she tilted her chin and looked up into the gipsy face above her. He was smiling, and his eyes, the colour of sea-water beneath the slanting black brows, teased and challenged her. She felt the full force of his daredevil charm, and could not wonder that so many women had surrendered to it.

"The world has so judged you, Sir Gilroy," she replied as coolly as she could, "and I accept its judgment."

For a moment longer he looked down at her in silence, and then he shook his head. "Dear liar," he said gently, "if in your heart you believed it, you would not dare to bait me thus." She felt his hands tighten upon her shoulders, and then with an odd little laugh he released her and turned abruptly away. "And if I were half the scoundrel you pretend to think me, you would have good cause now to be afraid."

With that he left her, and she heard him calling to Silas Birley that he wished to speak with him. They went into the tap-room, closing the door behind them, and after a little while Rowena made her way thoughtfully to her bed-chamber and sat down on the window-seat. Meditating upon Gil's parting words, she was obliged to admit that there was some truth in them, for in spite of her present circumstances she had no real fears for her own safety at his hands. All her doubts and suspicions were centered upon his association with Colonel Fury, and her dread of what might have befallen Peter.

She remained in her room until Tobias came to summon her to dinner, but when the meal was over she could not face the boredom of more solitary hours, and in spite of her resolution to keep Sir Gilroy at a frigid arm's-length, agreed to his suggestion that they should stroll in the garden behind the inn. When they returned to the house, Tobias had found somewhere a battered pack of cards, and with these they amused themselves

94

very tolerably until supper-time. When Rowena retired that night, she realised that the hours had slipped by uncommonly fast, and that she had found Sir Gilroy a pleasant and entertaining companion.

Patience came to attend her to bed, but they had scarcely reached her room when the sound of approaching horses came to jerk Rowena rudely back to reality, and to remind her that this was no ordinary inn, but the refuge and meeting-place of a notorious highwayman and his outlaw band. In spite of his arrangement with Gil the previous night, Colonel Fury had not since returned, but if this were he, then Rowena must find some means of learning what business they discussed.

As the riders dismounted before the inn, she knelt on the window-seat and peered downward through the tiny panes of thick glass which distorted everything beyond like images seen through water. She could see enough, however, to realise that neither of the newcomers was Colonel Fury. One was short and thick-set, in plain, dark riding-clothes, and the other—as the light from the parlour window fell upon him, Rowena uttered a stifled cry of joy and astonishment. She could not see his face, obscured from above by the broad brim of his hat, but there was no mistaking the tall, slight figure, the familiar brown velvet coat, the flowing curls and the hat with the saffron-coloured plume.

" 'Tis Peter!" she exclaimed, swinging round to Patience with flushed cheeks and shining eyes. "Oh, thank God, 'tis my brother, at last!"

She ran to the door and wrenched it open, and stumbled in darkness down the steep, winding stairs. She heard Patience call anxiously to her to stay, and then the other girl's light footsteps following her, but she paid no heed. Winged by relief and delight, she sped towards the open door of the tap-room, where lights burned now for the first time since she had entered the inn.

The two newcomers stood there in talk with Silas Birley, the man in the velvet coat with his back towards the door. She cried his name, then, even as he turned, flung herself impetuously into his arms, throwing her own about his neck.

" 'Peter', is it?" exclaimed a rough, astonished voice. "My name be William, but for a welcome such as this, my pretty, ye may call me any name ye choose!"

In dismay and disbelief, shocked to find herself imprisoned in a prompt embrace which was anything but brotherly, she looked up at the speaker for the first time. It was Peter's figure, Peter's familiar clothes, but the face between the curls of the periwig was that of a stranger, sallow and pock-marked, the lips grinning to reveal discoloured, broken teeth. The horror of it was too great to be borne, and in overwhelming terror she screamed again and again.

6

Dead Man's Shoes

At her first shriek William let her go and retreated a step or two, staring at her in astonishment and alarm. Dimly she was aware of his dismay and that of his companions, of Patience standing white-faced and uncertain in the doorway, most of all of her own screams ringing dementedly in her ears. It seemed beyond her power to check them. She was possessed and overwhelmed by the horror of this man with her brother's shape and clothes, but the ugly face of a stranger, and stood with her hands pressed to her cheeks, screaming like a madwoman.

The parlour door was wrenched open and Sir Gilroy strode across the narrow passage and into the taproom. His keen glance swept over the scene before him, lingered for a fraction of time upon William, and then passed with no change of expression to Rowena. He stepped up to her and, gripping her by the shoulders, shook her with a vigour almost brutal.

"Be silent!" he said sternly. "God's mercy! have you run mad?"

She stopped screaming and stood for a moment staring up at him, her eyes still dark with horror. Then she swayed forward and hid her face against his chest.

"Perhaps I have!" she whispered, "Oh, God! perhaps I have."

Still holding her, he looked above her bowed head at the silent people about him, and particularly at Tobias, who had come running at the sound of Rowena's cries and now stood beside Patience, staring unbelievingly at the man in the brown velvet coat. Gil's glance travelled in the same direction, and William, somewhat daunted by Mabyn's size and air of authority, said hastily:

"Damme if *I* know what ails the wench! First she throws herself into my arms, and then starts screeching as though I'd tried to ravish her."

"I thought it was Peter!" Rowena lifted an ashen face and spoke piteously. "I saw him from my window, and I was so thankful, so happy! I ran straight down to him, but when he turned round it was not Peter at all." Her voice broke, but she controlled it with a visible effort. "But those *are* Peter's clothes! I would know them anywhere! Oh, what has become of him?"

In William's unattractive countenance curiosity was suddenly replaced by alarm, which gave way as swiftly to a look of cunning. Exchanging a glance with his stout companion, he said with an uneasy laugh:

"Pox on't, the poor wench *is* mad! I've had this coat for a twelvemonth."

"Aye, that's so!" the stout man agreed stolidly "A twelvemonth at least."

"It is not true!" Rowena said with a sob. "Do you think I do not know my own brother's clothes when I see them? Sir Gilroy, *you* know I am right! You have seen Peter dressed thus often enough."

"I have seen him dressed in a similar fashion," Gil corrected her quietly. "You are consumed by anxiety for your brother, and when you caught a glimpse of someone bearing a chance likeness to him, you believed what you desired to believe."

"No!" She tore herself violently from his hold and backed away, staring at him with frightened eyes. "I am not mistaken, and you know it! You all know it!" She paused, looking from one to the other, seeing alarm, pity, suspicion, but no hint of a break in their conspiracy of silence. "You are all in league with each other, and with that devil who calls himself Colonel Fury! You have murdered my brother, and now parade like ghouls in a dead man's clothes. But you shall pay for it! I swear before God that you shall pay."

"Rowena, have done!" Gil's voice was harsh with what she took to be anger. "You are beside yourself, and know not what you say. I tell you that you are mistaken, and that the mere sight of a velvet coat and a saffron plume is small cause for a cry of murder. Now come away!"

He took her arm to lead her to the door, and for an instant she almost yielded to the command of voice and hand. Then her glance fell upon a pair of fringed and elaborately embroidered gloves which one of the strangers had dropped carelessly on to a nearby table. Her eyes widened, and she flung out an accusing hand.

"So I am mistaken, Sir Gilroy?" she cried with bitter mockery. "In the other garments, perhaps, but those gloves I embroidered myself as a gift for Peter. I can even tell you where upon the left gauntlet the threads are not perfectly matched. Do you dare now to say that I am mistaken?"

A little silence followed her words, a silence so tense with fear and suspicion that a quick-drawn breath would have shattered it. Then Gil said angrily:

"Gloves may be lost, or even stolen, but men do not kill each other over them. This grows wearisome, and an embarrassment to us all. Come!"

"No, I will not!" she said in a breaking voice. "You are in this as deep as they—deeper, for all I know! You and Colonel Fury . . ." she broke off with a gasp, for Gil, uttering an impatient oath, swept her up into his arms and carried her, despite her struggles, out of the room and across the passage to the parlour.

Tobias, following him, said anxiously: "Sir, Miss Rowena is right! Those gloves——"

"Quiet, you fool!" Gil set Rowena on her feet, but continued to hold her firmly. "Close that door!"

He waited until this command had been obeyed, and then led Rowena to one of the settles and made her sit down, beckoning to Tobias to come close. Seating himself beside the girl, he took her hand.

"Listen to me, both of you," he said quietly. "Of course you were not mistaken—I recognised Peter's clothes as well as you did. But it was madness to make such an outcry against Fury and his men in their own stronghold. If the charge be just, do you suppose that any of us will be permitted to leave this place alive?"

Tobias nodded grim agreement, but Rowena seemed scarcely to heed Gil's latter words. Her hand imprisoned in his, her eyes searching his face, she seemed to be pleading for reassurance from the man whom, a few moments before, she had been accusing of complicity in her brother's disappearance.

"You say 'if the charge be just'," she whispered. "Oh, tell me that you do not believe it is!"

"I hope with all my heart that it is not," he replied gravely, "but Peter did mean to return here, both to seek satisfaction from Fury, and to see Patience Birley again. Either reason were enough to cost him his life."

Rowena uttered a little cry of anguish and covered her eyes with her free hand. Tobias said in a shaking voice: "Why in God's name did Mr. Peter not tell *me* what he meant to do? For two of us there might have been a chance."

Gil shook his head. "No more for two than for one! Fury has a whole band of cut-throats at his command, and between them they must know every path and thicket on the Heath."

"You say that Peter returned here to see Patience Birley." Rowena took her hand from her eyes and looked up. She was very pale, but her voice was steady. "What is she to him?"

"One who sought to save his life," Gill replied. "He stumbled upon this place by chance, and she warned him of danger and sent him on his way. Later, it was her father who rescued him and carried him to the cottage, and then rode to London to bring you news of his plight."

She frowned. "The letter I received was penned by no common inn-keeper!"

"I fancy Silas Birley is the most *un*common inn-keeper we are ever likely to see," Gil said dryly. "Peter thought so, and though I scoffed then, now that

I have seen the man and his daughter, I am inclined to agree."

He broke off rather abruptly, but Rowena, her perception quickened by fear for her brother, guessed the thought which was in his mind.

"You would say, would you not, that it is one more reason to fear for Peter's safety in this place? Yet if they saved him once, surely they would not harm him when he came again?"

"They might not harm him, but who can tell whether they were able to save him a second time? Fury does not make the same mistake twice."

He paused, for the murmur of voices which had reached faintly to their ears from the tap-room grew suddenly louder, and footsteps rang on the stone floor of the passage. Gil rose to his feet and moved to the middle of the room, but the footsteps went past and out of the inn, and after a little came the sound of horses moving off. He shrugged slightly and abandoned his attitude of vigilance, but Rowena spoke in quick dismay.

"Those men have gone, and I discovered nothing."

"They would have told you nothing, any more than Fury himself would tell me when I questioned him last night."

"Then what am I to do?" She stared at him, still torn between her doubts of his honesty and her desperate need of his help. Need triumphed, and she stretched out her hand to him in a pleading gesture. "Sir Gilroy, help me! I *must* know the truth! No matter how bitter it may be, it cannot be worse than the torments of uncertainty which beset me now."

"I know!" He came to her at once, taking her hand

and drawing her to her feet. There was a gentleness in his voice, and in his dark face, which brought unwelcome tears to her eyes. "It may be that Birley can be persuaded to tell us what he knows. Will you leave me to question him? Go back to your room, and as soon as I have spoken with him, I will send Tobias to tell you what I have learned. Then, if need be, we will talk again."

For a little longer she regarded him uncertainly, and then she sighed and nodded. He led her across to the door and opened it, but then paused, looking down at her in silence, and she found that she could not withdraw her gaze from his. At length he said, too softly for Tobias to hear, and in a tone which, from a man so self-assured, seemed oddly entreating: "Trust me a little, Rowena!"

He did not wait for a reply, but released her hand and stepped aside so that she might go out of the room, though he stood watching her until she had passed from his sight around the bend of the stairs. Then he closed the door and came slowly back to Tobias, who saw that he looked uncommonly stern. He halted by the table and stood drumming his fingers upon it, apparently oblivious of his companion until Tobias asked bluntly:

"Is there any hope, sir, of finding Mr. Peter alive?"

Gil looked up. "I have none," he replied curtly, "and neither, I think, have you, but how could I tell his sister so? She may believe that she would rather know his fate, but in uncertainty there is at least a glimmer of hope. As long as she can cling to that, she will not break. Time enough for her to face the truth when she is safe home again."

Tobias nodded, but said grimly: "Pray God we may get her safely home! There's Colonel Fury to be reckoned with, and the two rogues who just rode away, and who knows how many more? Small chance we two would have against the whole pack of 'em."

"It must not come to that," Gil said curtly. "Somehow Miss Buckland must be carried to safety. I hoped that those two ruffians meant to spend the night here, for then we might have contrived to get possession of their horses."

Tobias's eyes gleamed appreciatively, but he merely said: "What of Master Birley, sir? If he helped Mr. Peter he might be ready to help Miss Rowena, too."

"It is possible! At all events, it will be well to know just where he stands. Peter suspected that he sheltered Fury against his will."

"That's my own feeling, sir, though he's said naught to me. Reckon he's one who knows how to keep his own counsel. Shall I bid him come to you?"

Gil nodded, but as Tobias went towards the door said suddenly: "No, wait! 'Tis an old truth that a chain is no stronger than its weakest link. Send the girl to me instead."

Tobias went off, and a few minutes later Patience came timidly into the parlour. Sir Gilroy was standing before the fireplace, his back to the hearth and his shoulders propped against the rough beam at his back. He looked down sardonically at the girl standing apprehensively before him.

"Patience," he said softly, "this night I have seen a rogue ripe for the gallows swaggering here in clothes belonging to my friend. Where lies he who should by right be wearing those garments?"

Her eyes, wide and frightened, lifted fleetingly to his face and then dropped again. She shook her head. "Your Honour," she said in a whisper, "I do not understand."

"You understand me very well, but let that pass. Why did you lie to Miss Buckland, telling her that you did not know her brother?" Again she shook her head, but before she could speak he went on sternly: "Denial is useless! Peter Buckland himself told me how he sought shelter here from a storm. Well?"

"Sir, we thought that if she found no news of him here she would go away."

"So that she would not discover that he was put to death beneath this roof?"

"No!" The denial came sharply, on a note of alarm, but then her voice dropped again. "For her own sake, that she might not come to harm. Surely you can see the peril which surrounds her? Only your presence has protected her thus far."

"I am aware of it!" A faint, contemptuous smile touched his lips. " 'Tis my belief, however, that your concern for her springs from the fear that she may divert Colonel Fury's attention from you."

She looked startled, then gave a little, mirthless laugh. "That is the last thing I fear."

"Yet you do not deny that you are his mistress?"

She averted her face, but could not conceal the burning flush which rose in her cheeks. "I cannot deny it," she said, so faintly that he had to bend his head to distinguish the words, "but 'tis a degradation which was forced upon me, and from which I long to be delivered."

There was a pause. Gil strolled across to the table

105

and poured wine into a glass, then, with it in his hand, turned to face the girl again.

"Excellently well done!" he said mockingly. "You would be a credit, mistress, to any troupe of players. Was that the tale with which you drew young Buckland into the snare?"

She stared at him for a moment, not comprehending, and then the painful colour faded from her face, leaving it as white as the broad linen collar which covered her shoulders. She made a little gesture of protest and denial, and Gil lifted the glass of wine in mock salutation.

"Vastly effective," he said with deepening irony, "but I happen to know, my girl, that a highwayman's doxy has to do more than amuse him during his idle hours. She works with him and for him, spying upon unwary travellers, or luring them into his clutches as you lured Peter Buckland—and no doubt many others. Are these duties also forced upon you?"

"I have never done these things! I do not deny that he commanded me to detain any wealthy traveller who halted here during his absence, but none come to so isolated a house. Mr. Buckland was the first, and him I sought to save. My father did save his life, at risk of his own."

"I am not speaking of Buckland's first visit here, but of the second. What befell him then? Or rather, *how* did it befall him? For I have no doubt that he was murdered here."

Patience gave a sob and covered her face with her hands. He studied her as though calculating the effect of his words, and then continued mercilessly:

"Murdered, and his body stripped before it was

flung into an unmarked grave! Who struck him down? That ruffian I saw just now? Or was Fury himself summoned to do the deed, as he was summoned last night by news of Miss Buckland's arrival?"

"We did not summon him!" Patience's voice came muffled between the masking hands. "I told you, we hoped that she would go when she learned nothing from us."

"But you did summon him to deal with Peter Buckland, the first time he came here?"

"Thomas, the stable-boy, rode to fetch him, but he is in Fury's pay, not ours. Even when they returned, I tried to deceive them into thinking that Peter had ridden towards Staines, and not towards Hounslow."

"Peter!" Gil repeated thoughtfully. "That name trips lightly from your tongue, mistress! It argues a closer acquaintance than the one brief meeting you would have me believe."

She lifted her head, her eyes wide with dismay, and then, as he put down the wine-glass he held and moved towards her, shrank from him in obvious alarm.

"Do not mistake me, mistress," he said softly. "Peter Buckland's death is a score which shall be settled by and by, but for the present it is his sister's safety which concerns me most of all. If any harm befalls her, I swear that I will have this thieves' den burned about your ears, and see every last one of you dead or thrown into prison. And do not think I threaten what I cannot perform."

Patience cowered against the settle beside her, apparently half fainting with terror, but somehow summoned up enough courage to reply. "We mean Miss

Buckland no harm, sir, but you are the only one who can save her."

Gil's eyes narrowed, and he said in a tone of quiet menace: "You trifle with me, I think! Had our horses not been stolen, I would have had her safe in her own home hours ago, but without mounts we are as good as prisoners here."

"We are all prisoners," she whispered hopelessly. "Father and I as much as the rest of you."

"So whines every criminal who sees justice threatening him," Gil retorted contemptuously, "but I am prepared to strike a bargain with you and your father. Help me to place Miss Buckland beyond Fury's reach, and when the reckoning comes, I will do what I can to save you. I am not without influence."

She shook her head. "It is no use! Please, sir, let me go! I cannot help you."

"Cannot?" he repeated. "Say 'will not', and you come closer to the truth! So be it, then, but remember! No court will believe your plea of innocence, any more than I believe it now, and necks just as soft and white as yours have felt the hangman's noose ere now." She uttered a choking gasp and pressed a hand to her throat, and the sneer deepened in the dark face watching her. "No doubt 'tis very fine to have the great Colonel Fury for your lover, but is your pleasure worth a ride to Tyburn? I would not have thought him the man to inspire such devotion!"

Slowly Patience lifted her head to look at him. She was still very pale, and now there was a bitterness in her face which robbed it of youth and beauty.

"Devotion?" she whispered. "Merciful God, what mockery!"

With a sudden, reckless gesture she tore off her wide linen collar and fumbled with the laces of her gown. Then, turning from him, she slipped the dress down from her shoulders, and his eyes narrowed at sight of the long, puckered scars which disfigured her back.

"I tried once to cheat him of his prey," she said in the same bitter, hopeless voice, "and that is what it earned me. He swears that next time he will lay the lash across my face. Do you still marvel that I am afraid to help you?"

The look of contempt had faded from Gil's eyes, and in its place was anger, the profound and deadly anger of a man whose temper was not easily roused. He who would take up a quarrel with a careless jest and fight with laughter on his lips was moved now by feelings which went beyond mockery and beyond mirth.

"He has not changed!" he said as though to himself. "No, by Heaven, he has not!" Then, more gently, he added: "But you need not fear that he will harm you again. Show me the way to convey Miss Buckland back to London, and you shall go with her, out of reach of his vengeance."

She shook her head. The brief mood of defiance had passed, and she dropped down in the corner of the settle, pressing her forehead against the high wooden back.

"It is no use," she said dully. "Even if I could escape, he holds over my father the power of life and death, and will use it if we seek to betray him. I dare not help you to have him brought to trial."

"That was not my meaning!" Gil's tone was grim. "Colonel Fury must not die by the rope, but by the sword."

"That is impossible!" Patience spoke hopelessly, not lifting her head. "Others have tried, and failed. Father says he is a master swordsman."

"I am willing to pit my skill against his, but I dare not risk my life while Miss Buckland depends upon me for protection. Until she is safe home again, my hands are tied. That is why you and your father must help me." She shook her head, and he moved to sit beside her where she crouched on the settle. Gripping her by the shoulders, he pulled her upright, speaking in a low, urgent voice. "Great gains demand some risk! Tell me how I may obtain horses, and I will rid you of Colonel Fury."

Before she could reply, a light footstep sounded in the passage and Rowena came into the room. She checked on the threshold, her eyes wide and disbelieving as she took in the scene before her, Patience with her dress in disarray, Gil holding her in what seemed to Rowena's outraged eyes to be an amorous embrace. After an instant of shock, a look of disgust came into her face and she said icily:

"I intrude, it seems! It would be more prudent, Sir Gilroy, to find some private place in which to pursue your—inquiries!" Then her cold scorn faltered, and her voice began to shake with an anger she could not control. "And do not dare to ask me again to trust you!"

7

The Inn-keeper's Tale

She swung round and away, slamming the door with a force which almost extinguished the candles. The two in the parlour heard her run along the passage and stumble as she mounted the stairs, and then from above the crash of another slamming door sounded like an echo of the first. Gil, who had sprung to his feet, swore emphatically, and Patience looked up at him in dismay.

"It is my fault," she said distressfully. "I will go to her, make her understand."

"No!" He spoke curtly. "She would not listen to you, and in any event it is of small importance at present. Her differences with me must await a more convenient season for their settlement."

He moved to the table and took up his unfinished glass of wine, while Patience hurriedly tidied her gown. For a few moments there was silence, and then he said:

"I am still waiting to be told where I may obtain those horses."

"I cannot tell you, sir, indeed I cannot," she replied

unsteadily. "The only ones that are ever stabled here belong to Colonèl Fury and his men."

He looked thoughtfully at her, and then nodded. "I think the time has come for me to speak with your father," he said decisively. "Will you be good enough to ask him to come to me?" She nodded obediently and got up, but as she went towards the door he added: "Remember, I desire you to say nothing to Miss Buckland. She is in no mood tonight to listen to reason, and I have suffered enough already in that quarter from well-meant meddling. When the time comes, I will make my peace with her in my own way."

She looked doubtful, but murmured an assurance of obedience and went out. Some minutes went by, but Gil, guessing that she was telling her father what had passed, waited patiently, making himself comfortable in the elbow-chair and pouring another glass of wine. At length Silas Birley came into the room.

The two men regarded each other measuringly, the courtier in his silk and velvet, lounging at the head of the table, and the inn-keeper, clad in sober homespun, standing humbly before him. Then Gil said pleasantly:

"Sit down, Master Birley, and take a glass of wine with me."

It was plain that whatever the other man had expected him to say, it was certainly not this. His eyes widened in astonishment, and he said questioningly: "Sir?"

Gil smiled faintly. "Let us have an end of pretence, my friend! I do not need to be told that, in spite of your present circumstances, you were not born to a life of inn-keeping. So let us deal honestly with one another."

For a moment longer Birley hesitated, and then he fetched another glass from the cupboard and sat down at the table, moving the candles to one side. Gil filled the glass and then lifted his own in salutation.

"To our better understanding, sir, and to the aid which I hope we may give each other."

"I will drink to that, Sir Gilroy, with a very good will," Birley replied. A subtle change had come over him, and he was no longer the inn-keeper unduly honoured by a guest, but one man of breeding conversing upon equal terms with another. When the toast had been drunk, he went on: "As to aid, however, I am not certain that I can give it. There are no horses to be had nearer than Hounslow. Seek them closer at hand, and Fury will know of it before you can throw a saddle across their backs."

Gil frowned. "Yet you obtained a horse, the night you rescued Peter Buckland."

"One of Fury's men lay here that night. I plied him with drink and took his horse while he slept. It was back in the stable before he rose next day, and if he guessed that it had been ridden hard, fear of Fury's anger kept him silent. But such a chance is unlikely to occur at present."

"Most certainly, since Fury plainly intends to keep us prisoner here," Gil agreed. "Would it be possible to cross the Heath on foot?"

"A man might do so, if he went in disguise," Birley replied dubiously, "but Fury has many spies, and the journey would be too dangerous for a gently-bred woman. Nor can I stand surety for Miss Buckland's safety should you leave her here. It shames me to confess it, but I am far from being master in my own house."

"So he holds us!" Gil commented, and shook his head. "I do not like it, my friend! 'Tis not my habit to sit meekly waiting while a trap is sprung upon me."

The inn-keeper studied him thoughtfully. "You bade me have done with pretence, Sir Gilroy, so I will tell you what is in my mind. When Colonel Fury was here last night, you did not seem to deal together as enemies."

"A just observation," Gil agreed calmly, "but tell me this. Who counts Colonel Fury as a friend?"

Birley's grim smile conceded the point. "None that I know of! Even those who regard him as their leader would not hesitate to betray him if they saw profit in it, and could be sure that he would not betray them in his turn. But he has made it his business to know the name and habits and favourite haunts of every robber on the Heath, and if he were brought to trial not one of them would be safe."

"And not they alone," Gil added in a hard voice. "I have no wish to see him stand trial, and neither, I believe, have you."

"I am in his power deeper than any. That man, Sir Gilroy, has been my evil genius for fifteen years."

Gil looked surprised. "So long?"

Birley nodded. "I fought for the King in the late wars, and afterwards joined with those Royalists who carried on the fight along the English highways. The man who now calls himself Colonel Fury was one of our number."

"Then you know his real name?" Gil leaned forward

to ask the question with quiet urgency, but the inn-keeper shook his head.

"No, for he always chose to surround himself with mystery. I did not know it then, and I do not know it now."

Gil relaxed again and took up his glass of wine. When he had drunk, he said: "When the King came into his own again, you must have been granted free pardon for turning highwayman under Cromwell, so that cannot be the source of Fury's power over you. But I am not seeking to probe your secrets. As for my own, all I can tell you is that he is my enemy, and that though I came here to try to make terms with him, I believe that none of us will know true peace of mind as long as he lives."

He paused, but for several moments the elder man continued to regard him in silence, his eyes searching the dark, intrepid face. What he read there seemed to reassure him, and to bring him to a decision.

"To see Colonel Fury dead, Sir Gilroy," he said in a low voice, "is the paramount desire of my life. Would to God I had shot him down the day he first set foot in this house!"

Gil's brows lifted, and he said coolly: "Why did you not?"

Birley did not reply at once, but his glance left Gil's face and passed to the sword which hung above the hearth. After a little he sighed.

"Because then I had not gauged the full measure of his infamy," he said heavily, "and kill in cold blood I could not, even a man who knew the secret of the past I had thought long dead." He looked directly at Gil again, and there was a quiet dignity in his bearing.

"You say that you do not seek to probe my secret, but I will tell it none the less. Thus you may know that I trust you, and that you may trust me."

Gil shrugged. "As you will, sir! But I cannot undertake to reveal my own secrets in return."

"Nor do I ask it, Sir Gilroy!" Birley paused to drain his glass, as though fortifying himself for the tale he was about to relate. "As I told you, I knew Colonel Fury long ago. Among the fraternity of the highway his boldness and brutality were a by-word, and though I never liked him, we were bound by our common loyalty to the King. On one occasion it so fell out that he and I, being hard pressed by pursuit, sought refuge at my home in Oxfordshire, where everyone, save my wife and the few loyal servants left to us, believed that I had fled into exile." He paused, staring at the candle-flames, and the lines upon his face seemed to become more deeply graven. "My wife was young and very fair, much as my daughter is today, and Fury made no secret of his admiration. I was thankful when I could safely speed him on his way. Soon afterward the truth of my supposed exile became known to the authorities."

"He betrayed you!" Gil's voice was flat, stating a fact rather than asking a question.

"Aye, though I did not know it then. I escaped capture only by the devotion of my body-servant, who had remained faithful through all my changing fortunes, and the pursuit drove us far from home and into hiding. After a time, anxiety for my wife and infant daughter prompted me to risk a return, and as we neared the end of our journey, we met with Colonel Fury. He was in an evil mood that night, and bade me

116

beware of riding home, for I would find my place there already filled by one of Cromwell's officers. Then he rode away, laughing, before I could fling the lie back in his teeth."

He broke off abruptly and got to his feet, moving away towards the window. Gil turned in his chair to watch him, but the elder man was beyond the circle of candlelight, his face in shadow. Out of the dimness his voice came quietly, fraught with remembered pain.

"When I reached my home, the servants sought to stay me, but I thrust them aside and went straight to my wife's bed-chamber." Again he broke off, and when he resumed, it seemed that each word was torn from him by some intolerable torture. "Fury, God forgive him, had spoken the truth!"

He paused, and for a few seconds the stillness of death was upon the room. The wind sighed drearily in the chimney, and far out across the Heath the bleating of sheep sounded like a cry of despair. Gil sat frowning before him, feeling the silence grow intolerable, yet knowing that there were no fitting words with which to break it.

"A kind of madness came upon me," the tormented voice resumed at last. "I drew my sword and, defenceless though they were, I killed them both, my faithless wife and her Roundhead lover. Then I left the house where I had been so foully betrayed, and rode away into the darkness. Dimly I was aware that my servant had followed me, but dawn was breaking before either of us drew rein. When he would have spoken, I cursed him and bade him begone, but he thrust his horse in front of mine and put aside his cloak, and I saw that he carried my little daughter in his arm."

The inn-keeper paused and came slowly towards the table again, and the light revealed his white and ravaged face. Sinking down upon the bench, he bowed his head upon his hands and, seated thus, told in weary, broken sentences of the long flight which had begun in that winter's dawn, and how during it the servant had been killed when his tired horse stumbled and threw him on the frozen ground. His master had dressed the body in his own clothes and set his signet ring on the dead finger, hoping that those who found it would believe that it was he who had died. At last, finding refuge at a lonely inn amid the outlaws' haven of Hounslow Heath, he had made the exchange of identity complete by taking the dead man's name of Silas Birley.

"This house was kept then by a young widow," he concluded, "and she gave me the help I so desperately needed. She cared for the child and somehow saved me from running mad, and in the fullness of time I married her. She was a loyal and loving wife to me, God rest her, until the day she died, and she loved my daughter as her own."

The broken voice ceased at last, and there was silence. Gil filled the two glasses and pushed one towards his companion.

"And no one ever discovered your secret?" he asked after a while.

Birley sighed and raised his head. "Even my own daughter did not know it, for she was too young to recall much of our flight, and when she grew older I told her simply that I had lost lands and fortune during the wars. Even her name I changed. She had been christened Diana after her mother, but when we came here I taught her to use instead the Puritan name of

Patience." He sighed again. "I never wholly gave up hope of making some adequate provision for her, and to that end I educated her and taught her the speech and manner becoming a lady of quality. So we dwelt here in peace until, one ill-omened day, Colonel Fury rode up to the door."

He fell silent and sat staring before him, his face twisted with bitterness and pain. The candles were burning low, and the crowding shadows seemed to quiver with malignant life, as though they embodied the pitiless cruelty of the man who had come out of the past to shatter another's hard-won peace. Gil's face was very stern as he said:

"No need to tell me more! He recognised you, and because of what he knows, you are forced to do his bidding. Yet is the danger so very great? Would it not need more than the word of a rogue like Fury to convict you of a crime committed fifteen years ago by a man supposedly dead?"

"Sir, I married my first wife against the wishes of her family, and that family has since grown powerful. One word to them that I am still alive, and they will not rest until they have seen me hang for her murder. Fury knows that as well as I do, and so has made me his lackey." He turned his head to look at Gil, and there was a terrible, mirthless mockery in his face. "When he threatened me, I played the coward for my daughter's sake, fearing what might befall her if I were taken. It could scarcely have been worse than what she has suffered at Fury's hands!"

"He must be killed!" Gil spoke without passion, as one stating an unarguable fact. "I only marvel that you have not shot him down like the beast of prey he is."

"Do not suppose I have not thought on it," Birley said bitterly, "but he has cheated me even of that. Since his coming, my house has become a meeting-place for every thieving rogue who haunts the Heath, and more than one of them covet both it and my daughter. Only fear of Fury holds them in check." His eyes met Gil's squarely, and he added in a deliberate voice: "I will give you any aid in my power, Sir Gilroy, if it means his death!"

"I intend to fight him," Gil said quietly, "but first the women must be placed in safety. Before we take thought on that, however, there is another matter of which we must speak. What of Peter Buckland? He did return here, did he not?"

"Yes, he returned!" Birley turned away as he spoke, his shoulders bowed as though by some grievous load. "Though I had counselled him to forget us, he came back to offer Patience his aid and protection. Fury found him here. That is all I am able to tell you."

"What need to say more?" Gil retorted bitterly. "Even in fair fight Peter would have been no match for such an adversary." He was silent for a space, and then sighed, as though thrusting aside vain regrets. "You were wise to deny all knowledge of him to his sister. Continue to do so! I will tell her the truth myself when the right moment comes."

8

Disenchantment

After her tempestuous return to her bedchamber, Rowena had cast herself down on the window-seat, shaking with an anger and a disgust directed as much against herself as against Sir Gilroy. What a fool she had been to allow herself to be swayed by his undeniable charm. She was well served by the fierce and painful emotion which gripped her now, and which she recognised with shocked dismay to be jealousy. It was the final humiliation.

Slowly, however, the heat of her righteous anger began to be tinged with an icy dread. Perhaps Gil had probed no further into the mystery of Peter's disappearance because he had no need to do so. Perhaps he was deeper in Colonel Fury's confidence than she had supposed, and Peter, having stumbled upon their secret, had been silenced before he could betray it. In her distress she had believed Gil's sympathy to be sincere, and if impatience and a burning anxiety for her brother had not driven her downstairs just now, she would have accepted without question whatever lies he chose to tell her.

She stared through the window at the dim expanse of the Heath lying still and silent under the moon, and a desperate resolve formed in her mind. Tomorrow she and Tobias would leave the inn, would slip out unobserved and endeavour to reach the high-road and seek help from some passing traveller. And if they were spared to reach London again, she would tell all she knew of Colonel Fury and Sir Gilroy Mabyn and the inn of the Seven Magpies. Would swear to it, if need be, before judge and jury.

The following morning found her in complete command of herself, and when Patience came timidly to help her to dress, she refused her attendance with a biting disdain which sent the other girl away in tears. Heartened by this triumph, Rowena went downstairs to the parlour determined to treat Sir Gilroy in the same manner, and somewhat to her surprise he took the hint. They breakfasted in chilly silence, waited upon by Silas Birley, and when the meal was over, Rowena got up, saying to the inn-keeper:

"I am going upstairs again. Pray bid Tobias come to me there."

He hesitated, and glanced quickly at Sir Gilroy before saying apologetically: "Madam, Master Thorne is no longer here!"

"Not here?" She repeated the words unbelievingly. "I do not understand."

"He left the house at dawn, Miss Buckland," Birley informed her civilly, and after staring at him for a moment she swung round upon Gil.

"This is your doing!" she exclaimed furiously. "What trickery are you plotting now?"

He signed to the inn-keeper to leave them, but

seemed to be in no haste to reply. Rowena waited with mingled anger and misgiving.

"Well?" she demanded at length. "Have you nothing to say, Sir Gilroy?"

Regarding her with an expression she could not fathom, he said quietly: "Would you believe me if I told you that I have sent Tobias for help?"

"No," she flashed, "I would not! Nothing could persuade him to leave me unprotected."

"Perhaps he believes *me* capable of giving you all the protection you need."

She thought of Tobias's unshaken and apparently unshakable trust in Sir Gilroy, and her uneasiness increased, but she said coldly: "That you are *capable* of protecting me I do not doubt, but even if you have cozened Tobias into thinking that you intend to do so, he would not willingly have left the inn with no word to me."

"Do you imagine that he would rouse you at daybreak to inform you of an intention you were bound to disapprove and forbid? For you would have forbidden it, would you not, when you knew that the suggestion came from me?"

Facing him across the littered table, from which he had risen when she did, she forced herself to look him full in the eyes. "Yes, Sir Gilroy," she said bitterly, "I would, for I cannot believe that any suggestion of yours would be prompted by sincere regard for me. Tobias was the only person in this accursed place upon whom I could depend. You urge me constantly to trust you, but words are easily spoken and yours as constantly belied by your actions."

He was silent, his gaze fixed upon her face, and to

her vexation she found that she could not sustain that thoughtful, penetrating regard. Obliged to look away, she tried to disguise the weakness by turning her back upon him and walking across to the window.

"I could endeavour to persuade you that you are wrong," he said at length, and to her amazement there was a faint note of contempt in his voice. "I could explain my actions and beg your forgiveness. But you would not believe me! Nor is it my custom to come as a suppliant to any woman. For your own sake I have tried to bring you reassurance, but since you will have none of it—why then, madam, you may believe what you choose!"

She did not deign to reply, but stared through the window at the uninviting scene beyond. The sky was dull and overcast, and the wind raised little clouds and eddies of dust from the barren earth. Remembering the project formed the previous night, she wondered whether she dare venture out alone into that forbidding waste, but it seemed that Sir Gilroy had an uncanny trick of reading her thoughts.

"If, as I suspect, you are contemplating flight," he remarked, "permit me to warn you against it. You would lose your way upon the Heath or fall prey to one of Fury's henchmen, and that is a risk I will not allow you to take."

"*You* will not allow!" Indignation brought her swinging round to face him. "Perhaps you mean to keep me here by force?"

"Certainly, if your stubbornness makes it necessary," he agreed pleasantly. "I can very easily lock you in your bedchamber or . . ." he paused, and a gleam of amusement crept into his eyes. "Or I could simply take away your shoes. Upon such stony ground you would not go very far without them."

She had no doubt that he would make good his threat if the need arose, and the prospect of such indignity she could not endure. Retreating strategically towards the door, she said with as much composure as she could muster:

"I have no intention of running away, since it is plain that it would avail me not at all. That you threaten to constrain me, however, merely convinces me that whatever I have heard to your discredit is but half the tale. Far from maligning you, Sir Gilroy, rumour credits you with virtues you do not possess!"

On that she left him, though not without a glimpse of the mocking bow with which he acknowledged the denunciation. She went back to her bed-chamber, and as the hours dragged by, her fears and perplexities increased. First Peter, and now Tobias, had vanished from the inn of the Seven Magpies. Was she to be the next? Colonel Fury had not returned, and though Sir Gilroy betrayed neither uneasiness nor impatience, she could not believe that he was content to wait humbly upon the whims of a man who might well be plotting any manner of treachery. That thought led to another, and for the first time she wondered with a stab of alarm what would become of her if any harm befell Gil. It was not a pleasant thought. She did not trust him, but she trusted Colonel Fury even less.

She was determined not to leave her room again, and when Patience came to summon her to dinner, demanded that the meal be brought to her there. The time crawled past on leaden feet, and she began to wonder how much more of this self-imposed, fear-tormented solitude she could endure.

Towards evening, sitting by the windows, she saw Sir Gilroy step out of the inn and stand for a few moments looking across the Heath. Then, wrapping his cloak about him against the strong and chilly breeze, he strolled off along the track in the direction of the Staines road. Rowena watched him pass out of sight around the edge of the clump of trees, and wondered whether there was any purpose in his going or whether he had merely grown weary of being confined to the house.

From this conjecture she was diverted a short while later by the sight of a rider approaching from the opposite direction. Her first thought was of Colonel Fury, and she felt a pang of alarm that he should have come while Sir Gilroy was out of the house. Then, as he drew nearer, she realised from his build and the saffron plume in his hat that this was the man whom, last night, she had mistaken for her brother. He dismounted, and tethered his horse to a ring in the wall before entering the inn. Some minutes passed, while footsteps and voices disturbed the normal silence of the house, and then Silas Birley came out and led the horse away in the direction of the stable.

Rowena, who had been kneeling on the window-seat, sank back on her heels and tapped a fingernail thoughtfully against her teeth. The man William was alone; he must have some knowledge of what had befallen Peter; Sir Gilroy was not in the house. It seemed an excellent opportunity to pursue her quest for the truth.

Suppressing a natural feeling of nervousness, and deliberately putting out of her mind Gil's warning of the

folly of challenging Fury's men in their own stronghold, she got up and went quietly to open the door. All
seemed deserted, and she crept along the landing to the
head of the stairs. As she reached it, and almost before
she had time to become aware of a footfall as stealthy
as her own ascending, William himself appeared round
the bend of the staircase.

Rowena recoiled with a gasp, and for an instant the
man seemed equally taken aback, but he recovered at
once and grinned ingratiatingly.

"Well met, mistress!" he said in a gruff whisper. "I
were looking for ye."

"For me?" Rowena was vexed to find her voice
trembling. "Why?"

"Are ye still wishful to find that brother o' yourn?"

"To find him?" She stared unbelievingly for a
moment, and then, forgetting her fears, caught him by
the arm. "You know where he is? You will take me to
him?"

"Aye, but speak soft! They think him dead, and if
old Birley learns otherwise he'll carry word to Fury
fast enough."

"But what happened to Peter? Why did he not come
home?"

William motioned to her to move away from the
head of the stairs and, following, thrust her into a
shadowy recess at the corner of the landing. He said,
quickly and quietly:

"Fury found the young spark wi' Patience Birley. He
ran him through, for no man lies wi' Fury's doxy and
lives to boast of it. He left your brother for dead and
bade me bury him, but when I came to do it, the lad
were still breathing. I carried him off to a place I

knows of and tended him as best I could, and so far I've kept him alive."

She eyed him suspiciously. "Why should you do all this for a stranger?"

William grinned again. "Because I had a score to settle wi' Fury. This were a safe way o' doing it, and I took the lad's clothes so that Fury'd think I stripped the corpse afore I buried it. But enough o' talking! Let's begone while we can!"

He took her by the arm, but Rowena, still clinging to some shreds of prudence, hung back and said uncertainly: "What of Sir Gilroy?"

"Him?" William grimaced, and then spat to indicate his opinion of Mabyn. "As well trust Fury himself! Didn't ye know they be old cronies?"

A cold hand seemed to clutch suddenly at Rowena's heart. In spite of everything, in defiance of sense and reason, she had cherished a secret, unacknowledged hope of Gil's honesty but now that hope was shattered. William could have no reason for lying, and if Fury's men knew Gil Mabyn for their leader's accomplice, then Gil himself had lied to her from the first.

"Will ye come, mistress?" William's impatient whisper roused her from her bitter thoughts. "I told your brother as you were here, and he begged me to fetch you to him. He be mortal sick."

He needed to say no more. The picture thus conjured up of Peter desperately ill and begging for her help drove bitterness and caution alike from Rowena's mind, and filled her instead with a burning desire to hurry to him as fast as she could.

"Yes, yes! I will come!" she said breathlessly. "Let us make haste lest Sir Gilroy return!"

William wasted no more time, but preceded her down the stairs, pausing to peer cautiously along the lower passage before beckoning to her to follow. Together they slipped out of the inn and hastened furtively to the stable yard beyond. Crossing this, they plunged into the shelter of the stable itself, where William's horse, still saddled, moved restively in its stall.

"I told Birley I were here to meet my comrade," the highwayman explained as he tightened the girths, "but he be a cunning old fox as'll soon grow suspicious."

"Will they not follow us?" Rowena asked anxiously, and he chuckled.

"They be welcome to try—on foot!" he retorted. "Once we be away 'tis small chance they'll have o' catching us."

A shadow darkened the doorway, and Gil's deep voice said shortly: "First make your escape! You laugh too soon, sirrah!"

William cursed and made a grab for his pistol, but Gil's weapon was already in his hand. There was a spurt of flame, a deafening explosion, and William spun round and dropped beneath the plunging hooves of the startled horse.

Rowena screamed and clapped her hands to her face, and when she looked up again Gil had moved forward into the stable, and she could see Patience and her father standing staring in the doorway. Gil went into the stall and began to soothe the horse, and when it was quiet again he backed it out and Silas Birley came forward to lead it into the yard.

Gil stood for a few seconds looking grimly down at William's body, and then he turned away and came to take Rowena by the arm. She, too, had been staring at the crumpled thing lying on the straw, but at his touch she started and looked up into his face, and realisation of the manner in which he had thwarted her stabbed through her numb horror.

"You killed him!" she whispered. "He came to help me, and killed him!" She wrenched herself from his hold and backed away, her voice rising. "Dear Heaven! is there no one who can deliver me from you?"

"If you believe that rogue meant to do so, you are more foolish than I supposed!" Gil spoke curtly, his voice rough with anger. "Had he succeeded in luring you away, you would not have lived an hour. I warned you last night of the danger you courted by accusing him."

"You warned me," she cried bitterly, "but who was there to warn me against you? Against the false friend, the faithless lover, the boon-companion of highwaymen? Against Sir Gilroy Mabyn, murderer?"

"You are beside yourself," he said coldly, "but we have no time to waste in idle bickering. Come!"

He took a pace towards her and put out his hand, but she struck it aside with all the strength at her command. "I will not stir one step with you!" she panted. "I would rather await here the return of Colonel Fury, for he, at least, makes no secret of his villainy."

"You speak without knowledge, like the spoiled and wilful child you are! You will come with me, Rowena, whether you wish it or no, so do not try my patience too far."

The threat was unmistakable, and with a wild idea

of escape—though escape from what she did not know—she tried to dart past him to the door. He was too quick for her, and, helpless in his grasp, she struggled furiously. Then, realising that physical resistance was useless, struck out instead with words.

"Let me go! Take your hands from me! I am no common tavern-wench for your fondling!"

She saw his lips tighten and his eyes grow hard, and knew a fierce satisfaction at having stung him. An instant later, however, her pleasure was shattered by his reply.

"No, you are not, but by Heaven! there are times when you behave like one. 'Tis time we made an end of this!"

Still holding her with one hand, he jerked at the fastening of his cloak, and swept the garment from his shoulders to hers, twisting its ample folds about her so deftly that her arms were imprisoned and she stood helpless. Then he picked her up and bore her out of the stable into the yard, where Silas Birley was still holding the bridle of William's horse. Gil tossed his burden up on to the animal's back with scant ceremony, mounted behind her, and looked down at the keeper.

"I killed that fellow and took his horse and you could do naught to stay me," he said briefly. "Tell Fury so if he blames you for our escape. I shall return. Tell him that also."

A nod to Birley, a swift smile for Patience, and he was away without waiting for a reply. He turned the horse southward towards the Staines road and spurred to a gallop, and Rowena, breathless and uncomfortable, was paid no more heed than if she had been a sack of grain. Her fierce anger subsided, to be replaced by wretchedness and the first stirring of alarm. Where were they bound? He might know of other hiding-places on the Heath, and she was completely at his mercy.

Even when they reached the high-road and turned along it in the direction of Hounslow, she dared not raise her hopes too high. Her mind was a confusion of fears and suspicions, and she did not know what to believe.

On reaching the high-road, Gil had moderated his reckless speed, and suddenly he drew rein altogether to listen intently. Rowena, too, strained her ears, and after a moment caught the message borne towards them by the wind. There were other riders approaching.

If she were in any doubt as to Gil's motive in carrying her off, his reaction to the sound served to increase her fears a hundredfold. Without hesitation he urged his horse off the road and into the concealment of a spreading thicket of tall gorse bushes some twenty yards away, from which, himself hidden, he could see anyone who passed.

Rowena herself could see nothing at all. Clamped by a grip of iron against Sir Gilroy's broad chest, her face buried in his coat and her nose tickled by the curls of his periwig, she had some difficulty in breathing, and no chance at all to call for help. For what seemed an eternity they waited thus, until the hoofbeats of the approaching horses sounded close at hand. Then suddenly Gil gave an exclamation of satisfaction and spurred forward again out of his hiding-place.

"Well met, my friend!" His greeting rang out clear

and gay, arousing fresh fears in Rowena's mind. "It seems that our luck has turned at last!"

He reined in again, and Rowena, finding herself held less tightly, lifted her head and shook the tumbled hair out of her eyes. They were upon the highway again, and confronting her was Tobias, mounted, and leading a second horse which bore a lady's saddle. While she blinked at him in joyful disbelief, Gil dismounted, lifted her down and set her on her feet.

"By God, sir!" Tobias was saying as he got down from his horse. "When you rode out from those bushes I thought 'twas Colonel Fury himself. I never looked to see you here."

"A chance of escape offered, and it seemed more prudent to ride to meet you than to await your return." Gil was addressing Tobias, but looking at Rowena. "Every minute gained adds to your chances of escape."

Rowena struggled out of the hampering cloak and let it fall as she took a step towards her servant. "I do not understand," she said. "Tobias, why did you go without telling me?"

" 'Twas Sir Gilroy's thought, Miss Rowena, to send me off disguised as a beggar, so that I might fetch horses for you and me. He'd not leave you himself lest Colonel Fury returned to the inn. As for not telling you, we reckoned that what you didn't know of, you couldn't argue over."

Rowena turned slowly towards Gil, a dozen emotions struggling for mastery in her breast, but before she could speak he said briskly to Tobias:

"Even though we have horses, we are still within Fury's domain, and Miss Buckland will not be safe until she is out of it. Be off with you, and make for London as fast as you can. Those are *my* orders to you, and if your mistress tries to countermand them, pay no heed."

Tobias chuckled his assent, and Gil turned to Rowena. He set his hands on her shoulders and, looking shamefacedly up at him, she saw that the laughter was back in his dark face and teasing, blue-green eyes.

"You know now that I spoke the truth this morning," he said lightly, "and I may prove to be equally honest in other matters also. Think on that, sweetheart, until we meet again in London."

He pulled her to him and kissed her as she had never been kissed in her life, so that the whole world seemed to spin dizzily away, and the hands she had lifted to thrust him off instead clung to him as to the only reality. Then he let her go, and was turning away when he caught sight of the cloak lying crumpled at their feet. Picking it up, he dropped it around her shoulders.

"You had best keep that," he said carelessly. "You will not be home until after dark, and I believe 'twill rain ere long."

He mounted his horse, and with a nod to Tobias rode off in the direction of the inn. Rowena stood staring after him, breathless and shaken, her hands tightly clenched.

"How dared he use me so!" she said in a trembling voice. "How dared he! Oh, how I hate him!"

Tobias regarded her indulgently. "That's as may be, Miss Rowena," he remarked, "but you can hate him as well riding homewards as standing there. Let's be off, for we're not out of danger yet!"

9

Newgate Gaol

Sir Gilroy's prophecy of rain was fulfilled soon after they passed Chiswick, and though it was no more than a light drizzle, Rowena was damp and tired and dispirited by the time she dismounted at the door of her home. The servants greeted her with astonishment, and Mrs. Marriott was equally surprised, though she had discretion enough to hold her tongue until she and Rowena were alone in the girl's bed-chamber. Then she said with as much indignation as she ever ventured to show:

"I am thankful to see you safe home at last, cousin, for I could not be easy when I learned that you had ridden off with only Master Thorne to attend you. I cannot think that such conduct pleased your brother, though, upon my soul, it seems he made no better provision for your journey home."

Rowena turned away, saying as steadily as she could: "I have not seen my brother."

"Not seen him?" Astonishment and dismay mingled in Mrs. Marriott's voice. "You said that you were going to join him."

Rowena unfastened Sir Gilroy's cloak and dropped it on to the carved chest which stood nearby. She felt suddenly exhausted, and unequal to making the lengthy and involved explanations which would be unavoidable if she gave the least hint of the truth. Sick at heart, tortured by doubts and fears for her brother more bitter than the most dreadful certainty, she could not bring herself to speak of it.

"I thought I knew where he was to be found," she said at length, "but I was mistaken. So I came home again."

Mrs. Marriott gaped at her, and then, as Rowena moved away, unbuttoning the coat of her riding-dress, she picked up the discarded cloak and shook it out. For a few seconds she contemplated the size of it, the fine cloth and silken lining, and then said in a tone half questioning, half accusing: "This is a man's cloak!"

Rowena stood stock still for an instant and drew a long, steadying breath. Then she walked back to Mrs. Marriott and took the garment out of her hands.

"It belongs to Sir Gilroy Mabyn," she said wearily. "Now in pity's name, cousin, let me be! I am tired unto death, and desire only food and sleep. I will talk to you in the morning."

Mrs. Marriott gave her a look which was both affronted and perturbed, and then withdrew with as much dignity as she could muster. Rowena stood for a little while lost in thought, absently clasping the cloak to her with both hands. Then, suddenly becoming aware of what she did, she flushed and tossed it impatiently on to the chest again.

A night's rest did much to restore, outwardly at least, her usual composure, though she continued to avoid the promised discussion with her duenna. She was in no mood for conversation. There was too much to think about, too many questions which still remained unanswered. Gil's parting words were constantly in her mind. She had misjudged him in one thing, so it was perhaps possible that she had been equally mistaken in believing him in league with Colonel Fury. Perhaps he had been caught up quite innocently, as she and Peter had been, in the highwayman's villainous activities.

So confused and inconclusive were her thoughts that it was almost a relief when, midway through the morning, they were interrupted by the arrival of John Somerton. He made no reference to her absence from home, and she realised with a faint sense of shock that he could not know of it. So much had happened at the Seven Magpies that she felt as though weeks had passed since she and Tobias set out in search of the place.

It was not long before she realised that her adventures had wrought certain changes in herself. Mr. Somerton's conversation, which she had hitherto regarded as a model of sobriety and good sense, seemed unaccountably tedious, and she could even detect in him a pomposity which had previously escaped her notice. He sensed her lack of interest in spite of the civil mask she endeavoured to place upon it, and in some chagrin cut his visit short. He was on the point of departure when, almost as an afterthought, he imparted a piece of information for which, had he but known it, she would have forgiven him a deal more than pomposity. Inquiring whether her brother was still away, and receiving an affirmative reply, he added:

"Then, madam, you may send him a trifle of news which should afford him an uncommon degree of satisfaction. Colonel Fury, the highwayman, was taken prisoner yesterday."

Rowena gasped and leaned forward, her hands tightening on the arms of her chair. "Are you certain of this, sir?"

"As certain as may be, madam! My servant told me of it, and he had it from one who saw the rogue brought into London. A big man, dark-visaged and dressed like a gentleman. Is not that how your brother described Colonel Fury?"

She nodded, biting her lip. "Yes, that is he, but I do not understand. How and where was he captured?"

Mr. Somerton shrugged. "The story runs that he stopped a coach on Hounslow Heath at dusk, and while he was relieving its occupants of their valuables, a considerable party of travellers came in sight. Colonel Fury, being alone, made off, the newcomers gave chase and after a considerable pursuit caught and surrounded him. They bound him to his horse and escorted him to London, and he lies now in Newgate Gaol."

"He surrendered without a fight?" Rowena asked incredulously.

"So I am told. It does not astonish me, for such braggart bullies are generally cowards at heart."

She thought of the man who had come swaggering into the parlour at the Seven Magpies. It was difficult to picture him yielding tamely to capture and certain death, and yet the story was too circumstantial to be dismissed as mere rumour. She rose from her chair and walked across to the window, her mind a turmoil of hopes and fears from which, after a few moments, one thought clearly emerged. She turned again to face Somerton and Mrs. Marriott, who were watching her in puzzled silence.

"Mr. Somerton," she said steadily, "I have a favour to beg of you. Will you escort me to Newgate?"

He gaped at her, too astonished to reply. Mrs. Marriott said shrilly: "To Newgate? Rowena, have you lost your wits?"

"No, I have not! I wish to see Colonel Fury." She read shocked disapproval in their eyes, and knew that she would have to disclose part of the truth. "Believe me, this is not mere vulgar curiosity. My brother has disappeared, and I have reason to believe that he went in search of Colonel Fury. Now Fury himself lies prisoner in Newgate, and he is the one man who can tell me whether Peter is alive or dead. I *must* speak with him."

It was not to be supposed that they would agree at once, but after a good deal of protest and argument she had her way. Her coach was summoned, and soon, with a palpably uneasy and reluctant Mr. Somerton at her side, she was being driven along the Strand towards the City. Mrs. Marriott should have accompanied them, but the prospect had reduced her to a state of hysteria and Rowena had been thankful enough to leave her behind. She had also been careful to let no word of her intention reach Tobias, for she felt sure that he would disapprove. Time enough for him to learn of it when it was done.

When she stood at last before the gloomy pile of the ancient gaol, even Rowena's heart failed her a little. Newgate! The very name carried the odour of death and despair, for like all prisons it was overcrowded, filthy and verminous, a spawning-ground for vice and disease, with a grim tradition reaching back through the centuries. It needed all her resolution not to turn back, not to flee in horror from a place which, so she had heard, was a very fair semblance of Hell.

It was easy enough to gain admittance, for the citizens of London often entertained themselves by contemplating the plight of the wretched inmates, but to reach a prisoner as important as Colonel Fury was less simple. In Newgate, money could purchase anything except freedom, but the gaolers were well aware of the value of this particular prize, and though Rowena had come well provided with gold, Mr. Somerton was of small assistance. At last, however, after gilding the palms of innumerable underlings, they found themselves in the presence of the Keeper of Newgate himself.

The Keeper was well used to receiving people who came to beg or to buy favours, but this tall, chestnut-haired girl in her rich gown of pale yellow satin and dull gold silken mantle was something out of the common way. He went so far as to rise in her presence, and to listen patiently to the request she had come to make. When he had heard it he chuckled, and gave her a knowing look.

"Colonel Fury, is it? Pox on't, mistress, you lose no time, for he's lain here but one night! Well, well! he's a gallant rogue, and I dare swear you are not the only pretty wench willing to make his last days pleasant for him."

Mr. Somerton uttered an exclamation of disgust, but Rowena, though her cheeks had darkened, met the leering glance unflinchingly and said in a steady voice: "Will you let me speak with him?"

"Aye, where's the harm, though I must needs come also to be sure you've no chance to smuggle him the means to escape. But I warn you, mistress, 'tis an arrogant devil as swears he's innocent, and that 'twill go hard wi' me for keeping him here."

Rowena had no difficulty in believing this, and it began to dawn upon her that she had been a fool to come. If Colonel Fury was protesting his innocence, he was not likely to admit, in the Keeper's presence, to knowledge of a man whom he had probably murdered. But he would undoubtedly recognise her, and that might lead to all manner of complications which until that moment she had not paused to consider.

It was too late, however, to turn back, and she was obliged to follow the Keeper out of his room, with the reluctant John Somerton at her heels. As they went in single file along the narrow, dirty stone passages she held her skirts up with one hand while with the other she pressed a scented handkerchief to her nose in an attempt to counteract the all-pervading prison-stench, but both actions were purely mechanical. Her mind was filled with deepening misgiving, and the knowledge that once again she had acted with undue impetuosity.

The Keeper halted at last before one of the heavy, iron-studded doors and inserted a key in the lock. It turned with a harsh sound, and as the door creaked open Rowena saw that beyond lay a small, dark room, with floor, walls and roof of stone and a tiny, heavily-barred window set high in one wall. A table, stool and bedstead of rough wood appeared to be its only furniture, and upon the dirty coverings of the bed a man was lying, his face not visible from where she stood. He was a big man, clad in shirt and breeches—a coat was flung carelessly across the table—and he lay very much at his ease, hands behind his head, and his long legs stretched out so that the booted feet, with heavy fetters about the ankles, extended beyond the end of the bed. Although he must have heard the door open he gave no sign, and did not even turn his head.

"Fury, ye insolent knave, here's a lady come seeking you!" the Keeper bawled in a voice which curiously blended bullying with jocularity. "Get to your feet, and give her a proper greeting."

"Devil take you—and her! There is only one lady I have any desire to see." The prisoner turned his head as he spoke, the lazy voice checked for one infinitesimal moment, and then he sprang to his feet with as much agility as the fetters allowed. "And by Heaven! this is she."

"Sir Gilroy!"

"Mabyn!"

Rowena's exclamation, and Somerton's, came simultaneously, but where the girl's voice held only horror, the man's mingled astonishment with accusation, and something else which might have been satisfaction. For a few seconds they all stood staring at each other, as motionless as figures in a tableau, and then Rowena thrust past the Keeper and ran forward with outstretched hands.

"Oh, what has happened? How come you here?"

"Well you may ask, for 'tis what I have been asking since yestre'en!" Gil caught her hands hard in his, and she saw with amazement that he was laughing. "Things have come to a pretty pass when a man may not cross

Hounslow Heath without being taken for a highway-man and flung into prison."

She stared at him in bewilderment, not knowing what to believe, but remembering Tobias's words when they met on the Heath the previous evening. He had mistaken Gil for Colonel Fury, and if Fury himself had evaded his pursuers and they had later encountered Gil, a similar mistake was possible. The same description could be applied to them both, and in the dusk Gil's violet-coloured coat might easily have been confused with Fury's claret velvet. And Gil had his own reasons for not wishing Fury to be brought to trial.

He was still holding both her hands and showing no inclination to release them, but Rowena was too concerned to care. To the Keeper she said urgently: "A terrible mistake has been made. This gentleman is Sir Gilroy Mabyn."

To her astonishment this did not have the effect she expected. The Keeper grinned and nodded.

"Aye, so he says! 'Tis not the first time a gentleman born's taken to the highway."

"But he is not Colonel Fury!" Her voice shook with anger and dismay. "Mr. Somerton, tell him!"

Somerton shrugged. "That he is Sir Gilroy Mabyn I can swear," he said spitefully, "but that is all. I have never seen Colonel Fury."

Rowena caught her breath in horrified dismay, but recovered quickly to retort: "I have!" Then she gasped again as Gil's fingers tightened agonisingly on hers in silent warning, and she hastily amended the declaration. "I have heard him most particularly described by my brother, who suffered grievously at Colonel

Fury's hands. Do you think he would have kept silent if the highwayman had been Sir Gilroy?"

"Or that I would have been fool enough so to maltreat the brother of the woman I mean to marry?" Gil murmured. "Come, Somerton, let honesty take precedence over jealousy."

Somerton flushed scarlet and looked as though he were in danger of choking. Then, controlling himself with a visible effort, he said to the Keeper: "I have told you the only thing of which I have certain knowledge. Your prisoner *is* Gilroy Mabyn. Whether or not he is also Colonel Fury remains to be seen. Miss Buckland, if you are ready to go now I will escort you home. If not, pray give me leave to withdraw."

Rowena freed her hands from Gil's and turned to face him. Her chin was up and her eyes bright with scorn. "I am not ready," she said coldly. "Go, and do not trouble yourself to approach me again."

For a few seconds he stood staring at her with anger and dismay, as though unwilling to believe that he had heard her correctly, and then he turned and strode off along the corridor. Gil sighed and shook his head in mock despair.

"Will you never learn prudence?" he asked resignedly. "This is neither the time nor the place so to dismiss your protector, for I fear our good friend yonder will not permit *me* to escort you home."

She brushed this impatiently aside, vexed by a levity she could not share. "It does not matter. My coach is at the gate." She turned to the Keeper, an interested spectator. "Pay no heed to Mr. Somerton. You cannot keep Sir Gilroy prisoner here. He is not Colonel Fury, and there are many who will swear to it."

"Maybe," the Keeper replied sceptically, "but until they do, mistress, our fine gentleman bides here. How do I know this tale was not concerted between the pair of you afore he was taken? 'Twould not be the first time a man's looked to his wench to get him out o' Newgate."

Rowena gasped, and then drew herself up, her eyes flashing. "You are insolent, sirrah! Do I look like a highwayman's doxy?"

The Keeper studied her admiringly. "Not like the common run o' doxies, you don't," he admitted, "but seems like Colonel Fury's no common highwayman."

An abrupt movement from Sir Gilroy distracted Rowena's attention. He had turned away so that she could not see his face, but his broad shoulders were shaking, and she regarded him with increasing wrath.

"Oh, 'tis all a great jest to you, is it not?" she said in a trembling voice. "You would be well served if I left you to rot here in Colonel Fury's place. Perhaps then you would find less cause for mirth."

He turned towards her again, and though his eyes were indeed brimming with laughter it was not directed against her. Rather did it invite her to share his own amusement at the situation, but though this disarmed her anger a little, it could not vanquish it altogether.

"I am an ingrate, and I know it," he said ruefully, taking her hand again, "but you cannot blame this fellow for refusing to release me upon your word alone. To the best of his knowledge I *am* Colonel Fury, and it would cost him dear if he let so notable a rogue escape!"

"What, then, must I do to secure your freedom?" she asked unsteadily. The irons he wore had clanked dismally as he moved, and the grim sound, combined with the atmosphere of the dark and dirty cell in which they stood, for some reason brought her close to tears. "You cannot, you must not stay here!"

"I'll own I have conceived no great liking for the place," he admitted lightly. "The truth will out as soon as I am brought to trial, but I had as lief not wait so long. My surest way to freedom is for the King to be informed of my plight. Will you carry word of it to Whitehall?"

"I will go at once," she replied, and pressed the fingers that held hers. "You may trust me!"

A smile touched the corners of his mouth. "I do, sweetheart, I do!" he said softly. "Therein lies the difference between us."

With an angry exclamation she pulled her hand away and went from the room without a backward glance. The Keeper followed her, the door slammed shut with a hollow, booming sound, and the key grated harshly in the lock, but Sir Gilroy seemed unperturbed by his melancholy surroundings. For a little while he stood there, and then he laughed softly and threw himself down again upon the bed, humming a love song beneath his breath.

10

By Royal Command

The Keeper, who had been impressed in spite of himself by his prisoner's easy talk of Whitehall and the King, escorted Rowena to her coach and was at some pains to point out that the mistake, if mistake it were, had not been of his making. A man said to be Colonel Fury had been delivered into his charge, and he had accepted him as such. He had no authority to release him.

Rowena assured him that she was certain Sir Gilroy would bear him no ill will, and, climbing thankfully into the coach, ordered the servants to take her immediately to Whitehall. Her thoughts and emotions were in an even worse state of confusion than before. She was convinced that Gil could have established his identity when he was first challenged, and that he had not done so simply to afford the highwayman an opportunity to escape. He accused her of not trusting him, yet how could she, when he went to such lengths to protect a man who might well be her brother's murderer?

As she approached Westminster again, these doubts

and self-questionings began to be replaced by misgivings. When she first came to London she had made her curtsy to the King, and had since been to Court on several occasions with her brother. She had not greatly enjoyed these visits. Country-bred, and accustomed to standards looked on as laughable at Whitehall, she had been shocked and disgusted by the licentious behaviour of those about the King, and even, though she would always respect the Crown, of the King himself. She had found herself the object of attentions which offended and frightened her, and the prospect of venturing alone into the Palace was a daunting one.

She found the vast, sprawling building as crowded as it always was, and soon realised that without help she had little hope of obtaining audience with the King. For some time she wandered uncertainly among the throng, seeking an acquaintance who might advise her, and at last, in one of the great galleries, was fortunate enough to catch sight of the Countess of Castlemaine. She could not claim acquaintance with her ladyship, but Sir Gilroy knew her well, and upon one of Rowena's visits to the Palace had insisted upon presenting her to the Royal mistress-in-chief. Rowena had resented the incident at the time, but now, as she hastened towards the Countess, could only be thankful for it. She did not pause to reflect how strange it was that she should be willing to beg favours from a woman she despised, for the sake of a man whom she professed to dislike and distrust. All she could think of was the foul, misery-laden atmosphere of Newgate, and the clash of fetters against a stone floor.

The story hurriedly poured out to her afforded Lady

Castlemaine a good deal of amusement, but when she had laughed her fill she bore Rowena off with her to the King. His Majesty and those about him found the fact of Gil's imprisonment as diverting as Lady Castlemaine had done, but on the whole their mirth was kindly enough. Sir Gilroy Mabyn was well liked.

"It seems that Sir Gilroy protests his innocence in vain," the Countess concluded, "since, if Miss Buckland is to be believed, he bears a close resemblance to the highwayman."

Rowena, who had hitherto remained in the background, now found herself the target of many curious glances, including the King's. Some of these were malicious, but Charles Stuart at least could not bring himself to look unkindly upon a pretty woman.

"Miss Buckland, then, is familiar with Colonel Fury?" he said questioningly.

"Your Majesty, I know that he is a big man, dark-complexioned and always richly dressed," Rowena replied diffidently.

A sardonic expression touched the King's lips below the thin line of moustache. "Od'sfish! the description fits many men, myself among them," he said with a laugh. "Tell us, Miss Buckland, how it comes that *you* bring us the news of Sir Gilroy's misadventure?"

It was plain that this question had occurred to others besides the King, and the company regarded Rowena expectantly. She felt the colour rise in her cheeks, but answered with quiet dignity:

"Sire, Colonel Fury robbed my brother, and then flogged him and left him bound to a gibbet-post on Hounslow Heath. Now Peter has disappeared, and I fear he went to seek vengeance for his humiliation.

When I heard that Colonel Fury had been made prisoner, I hoped that I might learn from him what had become of Peter. That is why I went to Newgate."

One of the gentlemen standing near the King leaned forward to murmur something in his ear. Charles nodded and chuckled.

"So you are the lady Sir Gilroy is to marry!" he remarked. "Od'sfish! that must have been a merry meeting when you found him in Newgate instead of the highwayman. But let it not be said that Charles Stuart ever stood in the path of love's fulfilment! He shall be released." He signed to one of those who stood about him. "Give order for it!"

Rowena's cheeks burned more hotly than before, but to her own astonishment she heard herself say: "Your Majesty's graciousness emboldens me to beg one other favour, for myself rather than for Sir Gilroy. May *I* be allowed to bear the news to Newgate?"

The King's smile grew broader. "Why, so you shall, and I warrant the messenger will make the tidings doubly welcome! And though Colonel Fury be still at liberty, God send you good news of your brother."

Thus dismissed, Rowena could only express her gratitude as best she could, and be thankful to find herself no longer the centre of attention. There was some delay before the order for Sir Gilroy's release was brought to her, but at last, for the second time that day, she was being driven in the direction of the City, with a gentleman of the Royal household, appointed by the King to escort her, riding beside the coach. When they reached Newgate he dismounted and came to speak to her.

"I will carry His Majesty's command to the Keeper

of the prison, madam," he said courteously, "for it is not likely that you wish to enter the place again. Sir Gilroy will be with you in a short while."

Rowena agreed thankfully to this, for she had shrunk from the prospect of venturing again into Newgate. She watched her companion disappear into the grim interior of the gaol and then tried to interest herself in what was going on in the busy street around her, but the thought she was trying to avoid refused to be held at bay. When the King spoke of her as Sir Gilroy's future wife, she had by her silence admitted it to be true, and though it would have been difficult to deny it then, to do so now would be almost impossible. She could see no way of escape save flight, and how could she leave London while Peter's fate was still uncertain? Moreover, even if she went home to Mereworth there was no certainty that Sir Gilroy would not follow her.

She did not have much time to indulge in these disquieting reflections, for even Newgate's bolts and bars yielded readily to the Royal command, and it was not long before Sir Gilroy and the other gentleman emerged into the street. They stood talking for a minute or two, and though she could not hear what was said she felt certain that it concerned herself, for both looked towards the coach. Then the other man laughed and clapped Gil on the shoulder before mounting his horse. He doffed his hat to Rowena as he passed and she bowed in return, watching him ride off along the street, and not looking at Gil as he sprang up into the coach and took his place beside her. For a few moments he did not speak, but as the coach lurched forward he took her hand and lifted it to his lips.

"My thanks to you, Rowena," he said quietly. "You place me very deeply in your debt."

This was Sir Gilroy in serious vein again, in the mood which made it most difficult for her to remember her antagonism towards him. Angry with herself, she pulled her hand away and said curtly, still not looking at him:

"Not so, Sir Gilroy! The debt was mine, and in helping you to freedom I venture to think I have paid it."

"The debt was yours?" he repeated questioningly, and she did not need to look at him to know that he was smiling. "I have no recollection of it."

"I mean the service you did me in rescuing me from the Seven Magpies. I realise now that I stood in danger there, and I ask your pardon for not believing you when you said that you had sent Tobias for help. I had no right to abuse you as I did."

"As I recall it, I did not spare *your* feelings," he replied. "I recall also that I urged you to consider that since my honesty was proven in that instance, you might accept it in other matters. Or had you forgotten that?"

How could she forget it? The memory of their parting on Hounslow Heath was still so vivid that the mere recollection of it brought a blush to her cheeks. She took refuge in indignation that he should remind her of it.

"As you say, sir, your honesty in that instance was proven," she said stiffly. "It has not been so in aught else."

"Is proof so needful?" he asked in a curious tone between a laugh and a sigh. "Why will you not trust me without it?"

"Why will you not tell me what binds you to Colonel Fury?" she countered swiftly. "The mystery, sir, is of your making, not mine."

"I cannot tell you!" Gil leaned back in the corner of the coach; his voice was flat. "Nor would I if I could! Since you are so blinded by prejudice that you must needs believe me base in all things unless I am proven otherwise—why then, madam, it is not for me to seek to open your eyes!"

"That is unjust! Do you deny that you deliberately let yourself be taken prisoner so that Colonel Fury might go free?"

"No," Gil agreed equably, "I do not deny it. As I rode back to the inn last night I met with Fury. His horse had gone lame and his pursuers were hard upon his heels, though not at that moment in sight. I gave him my horse, and rode off on his in the opposite direction to that which he was taking. When those who followed came up with me I denied that I was he, but in such tone that they would not believe it."

"And so found yourself in Newgate," Rowena added crossly, "where, to my mind, you deserved to stay!"

A swift smile lit his eyes for an instant. "That is a curious sentiment from one so prompt to secure my release," he remarked. "I will own that I did not expect Newgate. When they made me prisoner I looked to be taken before the local Justices. I fancy I might have convinced them that a mistake had been made."

Rowena studied him with curiosity and faint distress. "Does it not rest heavily upon your conscience that you prevented the capture of one who is known to be a thief and a murderer? Can anything justify permitting such a man to escape?"

"I think it can," Gil replied quietly. "Believe me, I know more of Fury's villainy than you can even guess, but if he were taken, the innocent would suffer also. I will go to any lengths to prevent that!"

"Have the innocent not suffered already?" she asked bitterly. "Of what crime was Peter guilty?"

His face darkened. "Of none, save folly," he said in a low voice, "and that I might have prevented had I been less impatient. I shall never cease to reproach myself on that score."

Rowena sat with bent head, looking down at her hands tightly clasped together in her lap. "He is dead, is he not?" she said faintly.

"I fear so!" Gil's voice was gentle, and there was compassion in his face as he looked at her, but she was still looking down and did not see it.

"I do not believe it!" she declared fiercely. "I will not abandon hope unless I am given undeniable evidence of his death. If need be I will go back to that accursed inn to seek it."

Gil frowned. "You are not to return to the Seven Magpies," he said with finality. "Do you understand me, Rowena? I will not have you putting yourself in such danger again."

She gasped and lifted her head defiantly. "*You* will not have it?" she said furiously. "What right have you to tell me what I may or may not do?"

"It is the right of any man to protect the woman he loves," he replied curtly, in a tone which was very far from loving. "Someone must check your waywardness! By the grace of God you escaped from Fury once, but there is no warranty that you would be equally fortunate a second time."

"You are exceedingly anxious to keep me from the place! Is it perhaps because of what I might yet discover there?"

"As far as your brother is concerned there is nothing to be discovered, save from Fury himself. Are you foolish enough to suppose yourself a match for him? As for Birley and his daughter, all they know is that Peter returned to the inn and Fury found him there."

This reference to Patience Birley was unfortunate. It reminded Rowena of the scene she had come upon in the inn parlour.

"So they would have me believe!" she said contemptuously. "Next you will be telling me that they are the innocents who will suffer if Colonel Fury stands trial for his crimes."

"They, among others," he agreed calmly, and she gave a short, angry laugh.

"The others, no doubt, including Sir Gilroy Mabyn among their number?"

"No," he said surprisingly. "There is little harm that Fury can do me. Only those whom I am concerned to protect."

"Such as Patience Birley, perhaps?"

"She is one of them, certainly." The teasing note had crept back into his voice, and she knew that if she turned to meet his eyes she would find them glinting with laughter. "There is hope for me yet, it seems! Such spite against poor Patience has the savour of jealousy."

"Jealousy!" She repeated the word in a choking voice, her rage the greater because the charge struck home. "Of her claim upon you, whatever it may be? Heaven defend me! Your conceit of yourself passes all imagination!"

She turned her shoulder towards him and fixed her attention upon the street along which they were passing, though she could not afterwards recall a single thing she had seen there. Gil made no reply, but leaned back in his own corner of the coach and studied her rigid figure and averted face with some amusement. So they proceeded in a chilly silence which was not broken until, as they neared the end of the Strand, Rowena inquired stiffly where Sir Gilroy desired to be set down.

"At the nearest point to my lodging which does not put you, madam, to the smallest inconvenience," he replied with an elaborate courtesy which was in itself a mockery. "His Majesty commands my immediate attendance, but I must be rid of the grime of Newgate before presenting myself at Whitehall."

"As you please, sir," she agreed indifferently. "Pray instruct my servants accordingly."

He murmured his thanks, and presently thrust his head from the window to call to the coachman to stop. Then, springing down into the road, he turned, and with one hand still upon the open door looked again at Rowena.

"Will you come with me to the Palace?" he asked softly.

Rowena, who had been gazing straight before her, turned sharply to look at him. Go with him to Whitehall, endure the jests and sly insinuations, be present when he learned, as he was certain to do, that she had by her silence accepted the fact of their coming marriage? After her recent words to him, she could imagine no greater humiliation.

"Does His Majesty command my presence?" she asked faintly.

Gil shook his head. "No," he admitted with a smile. "I ask it, very humbly. Do I need to tell you that my greatest pleasure lies in your company?"

Rowena gripped her hands tightly together. Oh, he could be persuasive when he chose, with his deep, caressing voice and smiling eyes, persuasive enough to turn any woman's head. But she would not be one of those who fell willing victim to his easy charm.

"Your humility, sir, is as questionable as your sincerity," she replied coldly, "and I trust neither. Pray be good enough to bid my coachman drive on."

He stepped back, bowing in rueful acceptance of the dismissal, and after a moment or two the coach moved forward again. Rowena sat twisting a fold of her silken mantle between her fingers, feeling curiously depressed and at odds with the world. All the efforts and adventure of the past few days had accomplished nothing, and she was conscious of an overwhelming sense of loneliness. It must, she supposed, spring from unwilling, unacknowledged acceptance of her brother's death.

When the coach drew up again before the house, she saw Tobias waiting anxiously at the door. She guessed that Mrs. Marriott had told him of her visit to Newgate, and as he came to help her to alight she sighed in anticipation of the expected scolding.

"Thank the Lord you have returned at last, Miss Rowena," he greeted her. "I have been half out of my wits with worry, not knowing what had become of you."

"I will tell you about it directly, Tobias," she said wearily, "and I have no doubt that *you* will consider it fortunate that I chose to go to Newgate, so do not take me to task!"

She turned towards the house and Tobias followed, neither paying any heed to a man who was making his way towards them along the street. He was tall and thin, dressed in shabby, ill-fitting clothes, and he walked very slowly with bowed head, leaning heavily upon a stout staff. Instead of skirting the coach-and-four which half filled the narrow street, he stumbled straight towards the space between it and the steps of the house, and Tobias flung out an arm to keep him back until Rowena had passed. The thrust, slight though it was, sent him staggering back against the wheel of the coach, clutching at it to prevent himself from falling.

" 'Slife!" he said in a gasping voice. "What manner of welcome is this?"

Rowena uttered a faint scream, and Tobias, after one instant of frozen disbelief, sprang forward to support the swaying figure. Incredible though it was, the voice, and the face now seen for the first time below the misshapen hat, were those of Peter himself.

11

End of a Mystery

He was changed almost beyond recognition, not merely by his preposterous attire but by the ashen pallor of his sunken features, and the dark shadows like bruises beneath his eyes. Yet it was Peter himself, for all that he looked like a walking ghost of his former self, and after the first moment of shock Rowena ran to clasp him in her arms, tears of thankfulness springing to her eyes.

"Peter!" she whispered. "My dearest brother! Oh, God be praised!"

"Best help him within, Miss Rowena," Tobias interposed practically. Nothing could rob the man of common sense, but the prosaic words were spoken in a voice shaking with emotion. "He is well-nigh exhausted."

She nodded, taking her brother's arm, and so with Rowena upon one side, and Tobias on the other, Peter moved slowly into the house, past the gaping servants and into the parlour. There he sank gratefully into a chair, while Mrs. Marriott fluttered anxiously about, and Tobias, after a searching look at his young master, went to fetch wine.

Very gently Rowena pulled off her brother's shapeless hat and smoothed the close-cropped hair, and he looked up at her with a faint, weary smile. For a moment they regarded each other and then she dropped to her knees beside him and taking his hands in hers, bowed her face upon them.

"Peter!" she whispered. "Peter, I feared that you were dead!"

"I have been very close to death," he replied gravely. "On the very day I parted from you I met with a grievous accident."

She lifted her head to look steadily at him. "You mean, do you not, that you met with Colonel Fury?"

His expression changed, grew wary, and his eyes avoided hers. "You may believe that if you choose."

Tobias came into the room again bearing wine and glasses. Rowena rose to her feet and looked at Mrs. Marriott.

"Will you leave us, cousin? There is much that we have to say to each other."

The widow, who was obviously consumed by curiosity, tried to protest, but Rowena was firm and shepherded her out of the room. Tobias poured the wine and carried a glass of it to Peter, who sipped it gratefully, while Rowena picked up the other glass before moving to a chair. She felt that she needed it.

For a few minutes there was silence, but when she saw that her brother was beginning to look less haggard, and that a tinge of colour was creeping back into his face, she said quietly: "There is no need for pretence between us, Peter. Tobias and I have been to the Seven Magpies."

She told him briefly how she had discovered the name of the inn and gone to look for him, and how Sir Gilroy had found her there. He listened with growing astonishment and dismay, and when she paused he shook his head.

"God be thanked Gil did find you at the inn, for you were mad ever to venture there. It sickens me to contemplate what would have befallen you had he not come. Perhaps this will persuade you to regard him more kindly."

"Peter, do you not understand? Sir Gilroy knows this highwayman, knows him well!"

Peter took another sip of wine, regarding her with a troubled frown. "I cannot believe it!"

"You have no choice but to believe it," she replied shortly. "Tobias will bear out what I say. We both saw them greet each other with familiarity, and besides, if Sir Gilroy has had no dealings with Fury in the past, why does he fear the consequences of his arrest so greatly that he offers him five thousand pounds to leave England?"

"Gil did that?" Peter said incredulously, and looked at Tobias as though hoping that he would deny it. "Surely you must be mistaken?"

"I heard him say as much to Fury, and when later I took him to task he did not deny it. He is concerned to protect the innocent! That is what he would have us believe, yet he will offer no explanation of his conduct. If I will not trust him without proof, he says, then I may believe what I choose."

"Aye, that is more in Gil's usual humour!" Peter's

voice was relieved. "There is some simple explanation, depend upon it, but it is like him to tease you thus. As for Fury, devil knows he is the blackest villain I have ever met, but there is no doubt that he is of gentle birth. Perhaps Gil knew him in the past, before he took to the highway."

"That's true enough," Tobias put in firmly, "and what is more, I'll swear they did not meet as friends. But if Sir Gilroy does have anything to fear from Fury's arrest we shall know it soon enough, now that the rogue is safe in Newgate."

"Fury in Newgate?" Peter's voice was sharp with a dismay too profound to be on Sir Gilroy's behalf alone. "When was he taken?"

"Last night!" Rowena said briefly. "As soon as I heard of it I went to Newgate to demand news of you, but it was Sir Gilroy whom I found imprisoned there." She paused, looking at them with bitter satisfaction. "He had allowed himself to be taken so that Fury might go free. And you say they are not friends!"

They both stared at her in complete stupefaction, not knowing what to make of this piece of news. Then Peter said, in a voice from which he strove in vain to erase all uneasiness: "Whatever the reason, he cannot be permitted to stay there. We must do something to assist him."

"Be easy! He is already at liberty!" Rowena spoke calmly, though her colour had risen a little. "I went to the King, who was gracious enough to order Sir Gilroy's immediate release. That is why I was so long away."

Tobias chuckled, and Peter regarded his sister with a quizzical expression. "You brook no delay, do you, even on behalf of one whom you so deeply distrust?"

"I was glad of an opportunity to repay the debt I owed him for protecting me at the Seven Magpies," she retorted angrily. "I dislike being under an obligation to anyone, and particularly to Sir Gilroy Mabyn." She saw that he was about to speak again, and went on hurriedly: "But we have talked enough of my adventures. Tell us instead what befell you. It was the man called William who saved you, was it not?"

Peter looked blank. "I know no William," he replied. "My life was saved by the quick wits of the man whom you know as Silas Birley, and by his daughter's devoted care."

Rowena's lips parted, but at first she could not command her voice. "You were at the inn?" she said at length in a strangled voice. "But why in the name of pity did they not tell me?"

"I must have left the place before you arrived there, for it has taken me the better part of four days to reach home. Remember that I have not long risen from a sickbed. I had to cross the Heath on foot to the cottage where you found me once before, and that exhausted me so much that I was obliged to rest for a day and a night before I could go on. Then 'twas a farm wagon as far as the outskirts of London, and afterwards on foot again until I reached home."

"They should have told me!" Rowena said angrily. "Had they done so when I first arrived at the inn, we could have followed you to the cottage and brought you home. Oh, the fools! What possessed them to lie to me as they did?"

"No doubt they thought it safer for all of us that you should not know the truth," Peter replied curtly. "They tricked Fury into believing that I was dead, and we should all have paid for it with our lives had he discovered that he had been duped. And it ill becomes you, Rowena, to speak so of those to whom I owe my escape."

"But what happened to you at the inn?" she asked impatiently. "You still have not told us that!"

"Something which no doubt I should have foreseen. While I was talking with Patience and her father, Fury walked in upon us. There was another man with him, a villainous-looking fellow with a broken nose. This time Fury was willing to meet me sword in hand, and while we fought, the other rogue held Patience and Birley at pistol-point." He shifted in his chair, looking a little shamefaced. "I had hopes of killing Fury, but he is a magnificent swordsman and I could not even defend myself against him. As I fell, I heard Patience scream. That is the last thing I remember.

"When I came to myself again I was lying on a palletbed in the cellar of the inn, and she was kneeling beside me. She told me that her father had been the first to reach me after Fury struck me down. He realised that I was still breathing, but had the wit to tell Fury that he had killed me outright, and in his conceit the rogue did not trouble himself to confirm it. He told Birley to strip my body and bury it, and then he and his henchman rode away."

"And Master Birley and Patience kept you hidden and nursed you back to health," Rowena said in a low voice. "But why do they aid and shelter Fury, yet go to such lengths to thwart him? And why did you say just now 'the man you know as Silas Birley'? Is that not his true name?"

"No," Peter said quietly. "He is Sir Daniel Hartland, a gentleman of Oxfordshire knighted by the late King for his valour in battle. I will tell you how and why he became the landlord of the Seven Magpies, but first I must have your promise of silence. 'Tis a story which must never become known."

Mystified and intrigued, his companions gave the required assurance, and he told them briefly the tale which the inn-keeper himself had recounted to Sir Gilroy two nights before. When he had done, he got unsteadily to his feet and stood leaning one hand on the back of the chair.

"We have talked long enough," he said with an air of authority. "As soon as I am into some fresh clothes I am for the inn again, and this time, Tobias, I shall be glad of your company."

"Peter, you cannot mean to return there!" Rowena's voice was sharp with dismay. "Are you determined to throw away your life?"

"I am determined to aid those who aided me," he replied. "Would you have it otherwise?"

"I would have you use a measure of prudence! Is there no other way to repay your debt? Send them money so that they may leave the inn and travel beyond Fury's reach."

He shook his head. "I promised to return at once," he said stubbornly, "as soon as I had obtained that for which I came. Weapons to deal with Fury, and a coach to carry Patience and her father to safety."

"If Fury were dead, surely they would be safe at the inn?"

"He is not the only outlaw upon Hounslow Heath,

and even if he were, that is no fitting life for people of gentle birth. I mean to bring them here."

"Here?" Rowena exclaimed angrily, and broke off. For a moment she struggled with her feelings, and then went on in a more controlled voice: "Yes, you are right! We owe them more than we can ever repay, and it is our duty to offer them shelter. I dare swear that after a little teaching I shall even be able to find some suitable position for Patience."

Even to herself the words sounded condescending, but she was totally unprepared for their effect on her brother. He looked at her with undisguised scorn, and said in a tone of voice she had never heard from him before:

"You will not be required to put yourself to so much trouble. I intend to marry Patience."

The words struck her with the force of a physical blow, and for some seconds she was incapable of speech. It did not seem possible that she had heard him aright. After a stunned silence, she said in an appalled voice:

"Marry her? Heaven defend us! Have you lost your wits?"

He shook his head, and a faint smile lit his eyes. "No," he said simply, "only my heart. I love her, Rowena!"

It was an overture of peace, a hand held out to end their quarrel almost before it had begun, but she deliberately ignored it. The shock of his announcement had been too great.

"What has love to do with marriage?" she said tartly. "The girl is dowerless, uneducated—"

"I am not obliged to look for a rich bride," he inter-

166

rupted curtly. "Her father has educated her, and she is as well-born as we!"

"Well-born?" Rowena's temper escaped her control altogether, and with it went the last shreds of discretion. "The daughter of a murderer and a wanton? The mistress of Colonel Fury, and of who knows how many others besides? God's mercy! will you set a strumpet in our mother's place?"

Peter's face, already white with weariness, turned whiter yet with anger. He strode forward and struck his sister sharply across the cheek with his open hand.

"Let me hear such words against her but once more upon your lips," he said in a low voice that shook with passion, "and as God sees me, we shall be as strangers henceforth!"

"Peace, now! Peace, the pair of you!" Tobias, his presence momentarily forgotten, recalled it to their notice with that sharply spoken rebuke. "Shame on you both for acting so!"

Peter turned back to the chair from which he had risen and dropped abruptly into it. The brief spurt of anger seemed to have taxed his strength to the uttermost. He was breathing heavily and there were beads of sweat on his brow.

" 'Tis Rowena who should feel shame for her spiteful tongue," he said bitterly. "She is determined to look down upon Patience from her own blameless pedestal."

"You have been too long at Court!" Rowena, one hand pressed to her smarting cheek, spoke in a trembling voice. "You have learned to look upon honour as a mockery, and a virtuous woman as an object of contempt."

"Do not compare Patience Hartland to the

courtesáns of Whitehall!" Peter said in a dangerous tone. "Remember, she was not fortunate enough to have Gil Mabyn at her side to protect her from Fury's lust. You should be giving thanks for your own safe deliverance, rather than condemning her for that which is no fault of hers."

Thrusting aside an uneasy conviction that he spoke the truth, Rowena deliberately recalled to her mind how she had found Gil and Patience together two nights before. The memory stabbed her with fresh hurt and humiliation, and she used it readily to strike back at her brother.

"And what means did Sir Gilroy himself use to compel her into his arms?" she demanded fiercely. "With my own eyes I saw him fondling and embracing your virtuous Patience, and she half unclad. Nor was there any evidence of force on his part, or unwillingness on hers."

At her first words Peter had leaned forward in his chair, his hands clenching hard on the carved wood of the arms, but after remaining thus for a moment he relaxed again and said flatly: "I do not believe it!"

"You say I lie?"

"I say you are mistaken!" He was silent for a space, narrowly regarding his sister, and then a look of comprehension came into his eyes. " 'Tis my belief that whatever you saw, or thought you saw, has been distorted in your mind by nothing more nor less than jealousy. You are not as indifferent to Gil as you would have us believe."

"Oh, you are insufferable!" Rowena sprang to her feet, tears of anger in her eyes. "I will listen to no more! But mark this, Peter! If you marry that woman, I will not live under the same roof as she!"

"It will not be asked of you," Peter said wearily. He appeared to have recovered his temper completely, and his calm refusal to believe her accusation, coupled as it was with a reading of her state of mind which came very near the truth, enraged her more than anger would have done. "You will marry Gil before my own wedding takes place—though what he wants with such a shrew passes my understanding! And spare any declarations that you will have none of him! I believe them as little as you do yourself."

For a few seconds longer Rowena faced him with flushed cheeks and heaving breast, and then with a choked exclamation she swung round and swept furiously from the room. Peter rested his head against the back of the chair and looked ruefully at his servant.

"I swear, Tobias, the past half-hour has wearied me more than the whole journey from Hounslow. I had nigh forgotten what a spitfire my sister can be. Let us hope that Sir Gilroy does not look to find peacefulness in marriage."

Tobias chuckled grimly. "He'll know how to tame her, sir, never fear! As for Miss Rowena herself, you let her be! She will come about when she has had time to reflect on't."

Tobias's judgment of his young mistress was sound. Rowena, alone in her bedchamber, soon began to consider her brother's announcement in a calmer frame of mind, even though the thought of it continued to fill her with repugnance. She certainly could not prevent him from marrying Patience if he had made up his mind to do so, and to persist in showing resentment could lead only to an estrangement between them. That was the last thing she desired, for he was doubly dear to her now that she had come so close to losing him.

His pronouncement that her own wedding should precede his she thrust to the back of her mind. It had become a matter of principle to continue to fight against the arbitrary disposal of her future even though her hopes of victory seemed steadily to diminish, but that was a problem which could for the moment be set aside. There were matters of greater urgency demanding her attention.

Of this she was very soon given confirmation, for Mrs. Marriott came bustling into the room to inform her that Peter had apparently taken leave of his senses. "Anyone can see that he should be in his bed, with a physician to attend him," the widow added in explanation, "but instead he has given order for fresh horses to be put to the coach, and says he is going out again as soon as he has changed his clothes. I beseech you, cousin, do your utmost to dissuade him!"

Rowena stared at her in dismay. She had for the moment forgotten Peter's avowed intention of returning immediately to the Seven Magpies, and the news that he was preparing to carry out his plan filled her with alarm. She put Mrs. Marriott aside and hurried to his room.

In his own clothes once more, his cropped head covered by a periwig, Peter looked more his normal self, though the lines of weariness in his pale face were painfully apparent. Rowena, mindful of his servant's presence and certain curiosity, said carefully:

"Peter, I beg of you, do not make this journey today. You are in sore need of rest. Wait at least until tomorrow."

Peter took his sword and sword-belt from the servant and put the baldrick over his head, settling it on his right shoulder. He shook his head.

"My business is urgent," he replied curtly. "It brooks no delay." To the man he added: "Get you below and see whether my orders have been carried out."

Rowena waited until they were alone, and then went to her brother's side and laid a hand on his arm. "This is madness, my dear," she said in a low voice. "If you could not prevail against Colonel Fury when you were in full possession of your strength, how can you hope to vanquish him now?"

"I have no intention of crossing swords with him again. He has not scrupled to shoot men down in cold blood, and I count it no shame to deal in like manner with him. Tobias goes with me, and Sir Daniel himself waits only to be armed. I shall not be obliged to face Fury alone."

"You cannot hope to reach the inn before nightfall, and 'tis doubly dangerous to cross the Heath after dark."

He shook his head. "Not necessarily! More people travel by daylight, and 'tis then the highwaymen are abroad."

"But if they are not abroad by night, they may well be at the inn. Suppose you come upon a whole gathering of them?"

"I am not fool enough to drive straight up to the door with no precautions at all. Now in the devil's name, Rowena, have done! You will not succeed in dissuading me."

She saw that this was the truth, and in desperation, snatching at the only thing she could think of which would make his venture less hazardous, said quickly: "Then I beg of you, send word to Sir Gilroy. Tell him what you intend and ask that he go with you."

He regarded her blankly. "Devil take it, girl, you are a very weather-vane for inconstancy! Not an hour since you were insisting that Gil is in league with Fury."

She made an impatient gesture. "There is some bond between them, I know, but he has as little desire as you that Fury should be taken prisoner. I would prefer you to carry your tale to the nearest Justice, but since you will not do that, I would have you seek help in the only possible quarter."

Peter was silent for a space, obviously considering her suggestion, and she began to hope that he would agree to it. Then he shook his head.

"No," he said firmly. "If Gil is informed he will ride off alone to the inn and deal with Fury in his own way. This is something which I must do myself!"

Rowena, swallowing her rising impatience, prepared to argue. Then, acting on a sudden impulse, said instead: "Then let *me* come with you!"

He looked startled, and then contemptuous. "So that you may insult and humiliate Patience? I thank you, no!"

She shook her head. "I will not insult her. I was shocked and angry when you spoke of marrying her, but I had no right to say what I did. Poor child, she is more to be pitied than blamed!"

He regarded her sceptically. "And her supposed amour with Gil?"

"Perhaps I *was* mistaken!" Rowena bit her lip, and a

flush darkened her cheeks. "And even if I were not, I have little doubt where the real fault lay. Sir Gilroy is—overpersuasive." She saw that her brother was about to speak, and added hurriedly: "Peter, you are in no state to make this journey alone. If you will take me with you, I swear that I will use Patience with all courtesy. It is even possible that she will be glad of a woman's company."

It was plain that this latter argument carried more weight with him than all the rest. She saw indecision in his eyes, and heard it in his voice as he said dubiously: "It is no fit venture for a woman."

"Nor for a sick man either," she said ruefully. "I fancy we are both mad!" He continued to regard her doubtfully, and she put out both her hands to him. "Will you forgive me, Peter? What I said was cruel and unjust, and I am ashamed of it!"

He took her hands and pressed them, looking gravely into her eyes. "I forgive you, Rowena! These past weeks have not been easy for you either."

"These past days have not," she said unsteadily, "but enough of this! I will go to make ready for the journey."

He agreed, and let her go, but Rowena had preparations to make which he did not suspect. Hurrying back to her own room, she fetched pen and paper, and then sent Mrs. Marriott in search of Tobias. He was busy about his master's affairs, and by the time he came to her Rowena was already sealing a hastily written letter.

"Tobias," she said abruptly, "I am coming with you to the inn, but before we depart I wish you to find a trusty messenger to carry this letter to Sir Gilroy. He was commanded to Whitehall, but if he is not there, then the messenger must search until he finds him, no matter how long it may take." She took up her pen again, but paused to look significantly at Tobias. "Peter does not agree with me, but it is in my mind that we need help in what we go to do."

"My own thought exactly, Miss Rowena," he agreed grimly. "Praise be you have realised at last that Sir Gilroy is to be depended upon!"

She wrote the superscription with a flourish and held the letter out to him, looking up at him defiantly. "I still do not trust him," she said with some heat, "nor will I until I know what it is that binds him to this highwayman. He says that he is concerned to protect the innocent! Let him prove his words by coming to our aid!"

12 —

The Snare

They made the journey to Hounslow in good time and without any misadventure. The rain which had fallen the previous night had been too slight to make any impression upon a countryside parched by the summer sun, and Rowena, who had been hoping for weather bad enough to halt them, or at least to delay them until Sir Gilroy arrived, watched with dismay as the sun set in a cloudless sky. Its rosy glow was fading by the time they reached Hounslow, and when in desperation she suggested that they should halt there for supper, Peter brushed the suggestion scornfully aside.

"We will leave the coach at one of the inns and go the rest of the way on horseback," he added. "It will be better if the servants know nothing of our errand."

Rowena studied him anxiously. "Peter, you are not strong enough to ride! Even travelling thus has wearied you almost beyond endurance. Do not deny it, for I can read it in your face."

"I will contrive," he said obstinately. "The coach is too slow and cumbersome. It would betray us before ever we reached the inn, nor could we conceal it even if we arrived there undetected. Besides, if we are obliged to take flight, our chances of escape will be greater on horseback. We can take mounts with us for Patience and her father."

From this resolve nothing could shake him, even when they halted in the town, and Tobias, who had been riding beside the coach, came to add his protests to Rowena's. Peter was adamant, and would only relent sufficiently to agree that it might perhaps be wise to pause long enough to snatch a hasty meal. Rowena, determined to turn even this small concession to her own advantage, lingered over the food for as long as she dared, until Peter said impatiently that if she did not make haste he would go on without her.

"It would be more prudent to do so in any event," he added. "You will be safe here, and Tobias and I will make better speed without you."

"I will engage to ride mile for mile with you any day, even when you are in full health," she retorted hotly. She could see no point in remaining in Hounslow in the hope of intercepting Sir Gilroy, since, even if she did so, he would certainly not allow her to go with him to the Seven Magpies. "I am coming with you to the inn, and if you leave me here I shall immediately set out after you on my own."

Peter sighed, and pushed his plate away with its contents scarcely tasted. A weakness which he had been trying to ignore was dragging at him, his half-healed wound plagued him more and more with each passing hour, and he was bone-weary, too weary by far to argue with his forceful sister. Only the thought of Patience, and his stubborn determination to return to her that night, enabled him to go on.

"Oh, very well," he said heavily, "though why you are so eager to return to the damned place is more than I can understand! I should have thought that having once escaped from it, you would not wish to set eyes on it again."

Rowena made no reply. She was by no means eager to return to the Seven Magpies, but she feared that Peter's strength would fail him before the goal was reached. If that happened she would have to stay with him in some makeshift hiding-place while Tobias rode on to fetch Sir Daniel and his daughter. She knew her brother well enough to realise that he would never abandon the quest until Patience was safely beside him again.

So she assured herself, and tried to pretend that another and more pressing reason did not exist. At the Seven Magpies she might find the answer to the mystery of Sir Gilroy Mabyn's strange association with Colonel Fury, an answer which she had been fearing yet longing to find for the past three days. It had become the most important thing in the world to her, transcending even her anxiety for Peter.

So presently all three of them rode together out of the little town. Tobias was leading only one spare horse, for they had decided that it would be better for Patience to make the journey to Hounslow seated behind him than upon a mount of her own. She was unused to horseback, and there might be some hard riding to do before the night was over.

Twilight had deepened to darkness, but a full moon was rising, flooding the desolate landscape with a silvery radiance. Thickets of gorse and bramble sprawled as menacingly as crouching beasts, and now and then the three riders passed gibbets which reared against the luminous sky like ghastly parodies of trees. The night was warm, but Rowena shivered and drew her cloak more closely about her over the yellow satin gown. She wished now that she had worn riding-dress, or even borrowed a suit of Peter's clothes and disguised herself as a boy. It might then have been easier to maintain a show of boldness.

Save for the wandering flocks of sheep it seemed that they had the Heath to themselves, but when they came in sight of the clump of trees by the inn, Peter drew rein and said softly:

"We will leave the track now and circle round to approach the house from the rear. Thus we shall be able to conceal the horses among the trees, and you, Rowena, had best stay with them."

She let this pass in silence, for she had not come so far upon the journey to wait meekly in the background at the end of it. They tethered the horses, and Rowena followed the two men between the trees until they could all look down the slope of the little garden to the inn itself. The low, rambling house, with the stable to the left and a group of ramshackle outbuildings to the right, was dark and apparently deserted, though a light burned feebly in the kitchen. Peter had just begun to whisper to Tobias to approach the house in the shelter of the hedge surrounding the garden when the stillness was shattered by the sound of a pistol-shot from the direction of the house. Then, as the echoes died away, a woman screamed once, a high, shrill cry of terror and despair.

For a second or two the watchers among the trees stood petrified, in a silence which seemed the deeper now for having been so violently broken. Then Peter said in a stifled voice:

"Patience!"

He thrust his way boldly through the straggling hedge and went at a stumbling run down the sloping garden. Tobias cursed and, pausing only to tell Rowena sharply to stay where she was, limped after his young master, dragging a pistol from his belt as he went. Rowena paid no heed to the command, but, careless of thorny branches that tore at her gown, struggled through the gap in the hedge and ran as fast as her trailing skirts and trembling limbs allowed towards the house.

A door from the garden opened directly upon the big kitchen, and when she reached the threshold she thought for a moment that, save for her brother and Tobias, the room was empty. Then as she moved forward she saw the inn-keeper lying on his back before the great fireplace, his arms outflung and a red stain on his breast. A scream rose in her throat, but she choked it back and clutched at the table for support, fighting against the faintness which threatened to overwhelm her. Dimly she heard Tobias say:

"He is dead, God rest him, but whoever fired that shot must still be close at hand. Have a care, Mr. Peter, for the love of Heaven!"

The brief darkness cleared from Rowena's eyes and she found herself staring down at the interrupted preparations of a meal which littered the table. Vegetables and herbs were scattered there, and among them lay a small, sharp knife with a bone handle and narrow, pointed blade. Scarcely aware of what she did, conscious only of growing fear and the desire for a weapon, however small, with which to protect herself should the need arise, she snatched it up and, wrapping her handkerchief about the blade, thrust it into the pocket hidden in the folds of her skirt.

Tobias came to her side and grasped her arm with his free hand, while Peter, gripping a pistol, remained standing beside Hartland's body. Thus they waited and listened for they knew not what. Its customary silence had settled over the old inn. The door leading to the front of the house was shut, the outer one still stood open to the placid, moon-drenched garden, and from neither direction came any sound, any indication of another human presence. Had it not been for the body sprawling beside the fire, they might have supposed they had imagined that sudden shot and the cry which had followed it.

The seconds crawled by with mounting, unendurable tension, until Rowena felt that she must scream aloud. Then from behind the closed door came a faint, scuffling sound, the door itself crashed open beneath the impact of a booted foot, and framed in the opening stood Colonel Fury himself, holding Patience before him. She seemed to be half swooning, supported by the highwayman's left arm which gripped her hard against him, her back against his chest. In his right hand he held a pistol, its muzzle pressed firmly against the girl's temple.

Peter had swung round at the first sound, and now took a hasty step forward, uttering her name in a choking voice. Fury laughed on a jeering note.

"Do not move, my friend!" he said harshly. "One more step towards me, and Patience goes the same road as her father."

There was a furtive movement in the garden, and a lanky youth with a pistol in one hand and a coil of rope in the other came into the room. Fury nodded to him.

"A snare neatly sprung, Thomas! Take their weapons, and then bind their arms."

While this order was obeyed he waited, still holding his prisoner in the same position. Her eyes turned once to the motionless figure by the hearth and a shuddering moan broke from her lips, but then her gaze shifted to Peter and remained fixed upon his face. She seemed incapable of speech.

When Tobias and Peter had been disarmed, and their arms, and Rowena's, bound to their sides, Fury loosened his hold on Patience and gave her a shove that sent her sprawling at Thomas's feet.

"Bind her also," he ordered him. "I want them all secure."

Thomas obeyed, and then hoisted Patience to her feet again, while Colonel Fury put up his pistol and regarded his prisoners with grim satisfaction. Then he took up the candle from the table and jerked his head towards the door by which he had entered.

"Bring them into the parlour," he told Thomas. "'Tis more convenient for what I have in mind. Bring the rope also."

He turned and strode off along the passage, and with Thomas and his pistol behind them they had no choice but to follow. Coming to the parlour, they were herded towards the settles, Rowena and Peter to one, Tobias and Patience facing them on the other, while Fury lit more candles and then flung himself into the chair at the head of the table. From this position he was able to study all four of his captives, and a sneering smile touched his lips.

"A merry party, by my faith!" he remarked sardonically. "You should have learned by now, all of you, that I am not so easily bested." He paused, eyeing them reflectively, and then beckoned Thomas forward again. "We will have the men bound by the legs also, I think, for I am disposed to take no risks tonight."

Hurriedly but efficiently the order was obeyed, and then Thomas, still kneeling at Peter's feet, looked up at the highwayman to ask obsequiously: "Be there aught else, Colonel?"

"Aye, fetch me some wine, and be sure 'tis the best!"

The youth hurried out and silence descended upon the room. Patience was weeping soundlessly, the tears running down her cheeks and dropping on to the broad collar of her gown, while beside her Tobias sat rigidly erect. Rowena looked from one to the other and then turned her head towards Peter. He was slumped in the corner of the settle, his face white and haggard, with closed eyes. It seemed that he was stunned by this fresh disaster, by the effortless oversetting of all his hopes and plans. Last of all she looked at Colonel Fury, and found his dark gaze fixed upon her with the same insolent appraisal she had seen in it at their first meeting. A dull weight of fear pressed sickeningly upon her, but she dissembled it and stared defiantly back at him.

"What do you intend by us?" she demanded, and was gratified to hear her own voice clear and haughty.

The highwayman grinned at her. "You shall know that in due course. Our party is not yet complete, for

182

two guests have still to arrive. One of them is the messenger whom I sent to obtain for me certain information, and whom I look to meet here tonight."

Thomas came back into the room with a bottle of wine, fetched a glass from the cupboard, and set both before his leader. Fury poured himself a brimming measure.

"To your bright eyes, my dear," he said mockingly to Rowena, "and to our better acquaintance!"

Peter raised his head to say with an obvious effort: "Who else do you look to see here tonight?"

"Who?" Fury repeated. "Why, who but Sir Gilroy Mabyn? He should have convinced the authorities by now that he is not Colonel Fury, and he will lose no time in returning."

"If you expect him to follow *us* you are likely to be disappointed," Peter retorted. "He does not know that we are here."

"No?" Fury's glance returned to Rowena, noting her sudden pallor, her quickened breathing. "Your sister, Buckland, seems less certain of that. I do not think she would have come back here without informing Mabyn of her intention."

"What?" Peter turned his head to look at her. "God's pity, Rowena! You did not do such a thing?"

"If I had," she replied with a desperate attempt at evasion, "do you imagine that I would confess to it before this villain?"

Fury laughed softly. "It matters not whether you did so or not," he informed her. "Gil Mabyn and I have a trifle of business to settle, and he will return here for that purpose as soon as he is able. I think he will come tonight, and I have taken some pains to ensure that he receives a fitting welcome." He paused, studying her dismayed and puzzled face, and then laughed again. "Have you not guessed, any of you, how it was that you did not take me unprepared? I expect Gil Mabyn, and have seen to it that I am given warning of his coming. No matter from which direction he chooses to approach, I shall have knowledge of it, just as I was informed of your coming. My men know the Heath as you know the rooms of your own home and can cross it arrow-straight by day or by night."

"The inn at Hounslow!" It was Tobias who spoke, in a tone of concentrated anger and self-reproach. "I should have guessed that someone there would be in your pay!"

"You should indeed, particularly since you were prudent enough to go so much farther afield yesterday in your search for horses!" Fury took another pull at his wine. "I have not evaded capture, and taken such booty all this while by mere good luck. 'Tis costly to bribe so many, but it shows a rare profit." He turned to Thomas, who all this while had remained slouching against the wall beside the door. "And I do not pay you, sirrah, to idle there! Shutter the windows and bar all the doors save the one at the front of the house, and then get back to your post. I wish to know when Mabyn approaches and to leave him no choice as to the way he enters." He swallowed the rest of his wine and reached again for the bottle. "This time that insolent young devil will find that *I* am master here."

Rowena stared at him, but seemed to see instead Sir Daniel Hartland lying murdered upon his own hearthstone. He must have been unarmed, for Peter had said he had no pistols, and his sword hung still in its accustomed place above the hearth, yet Fury had shot him down without mercy. Were they to see Gil done to death with equal cold-bloodedness as soon as he set foot in the house? The possibility of it, coupled with the knowledge that it would be her plea for help which brought him there, was suddenly more than she could bear.

She closed her eyes, fighting against the anguish the thought invoked, and trying to convince herself that the horror she feared would not come to pass. When she opened them again, Thomas had gone. Only Colonel Fury remained, stretched at his ease in the big chair, his left hand thrust deep into his pocket, the right resting on the table with the fingers curved about his glass. He was not looking at her, and for a space she studied his cruel, arrogant face, searching it in vain for some redeeming feature.

Who was he? she wondered. Did anyone share the secret of the identity hidden beneath the flamboyant sobriquet of Colonel Fury? Sir Daniel had not discovered it in fifteen years, and even Gil had given no indication of knowing it. The highwayman was a figure of mystery, a malevolent shadow which brooded over them, threatening peace and happiness and even life itself, but of the substance behind the shadow they knew nothing.

As though becoming aware of her intent regard, he turned his head to look at her. For a second or two the dark gaze held hers, and then he laughed and picked up his glass again.

"The tide of good fortune runs strong for me tonight!" he remarked. "I awaited one enemy, and behold! Three more are delivered into my hands, even one whom I believed to be already rotting underground. 'Twas a neat trick the old man played on me, Buckland, when he told me that you were dead. I never doubted him until tonight, when Thomas came to me in mortal terror and swore that he had seen a dead man walking."

Peter shifted his position on the settle in a vain attempt to ease his discomfort. "Was that why you murdered Sir Daniel?" he asked contemptuously, though in a voice faint with weariness.

"No!" Fury reached out for the wine and filled his glass again. He seemed quite willing to talk. "My intention was to hold him and Patience hostage against your arrival, but he was fool enough to try to overpower me."

"My father deliberately threw his life away!" Patience spoke for the first time, her voice choked and trembling with tears. "He knew that you would kill him, but he hoped that the sound of the shot would warn Peter that all was not well."

"Instead of which it brought him blundering into the trap, intent upon rescuing you," Fury added brutally. " 'Tis a singularly inept champion you have chosen, my girl, though, by my faith, it seems that Gil Mabyn himself is like to fare no better this night!" He looked at Rowena. "For that he may thank you, madam! Your meddling has hampered him at every turn."

She knew that the accusation was justified. The knowledge was like a knife in her heart, but she scorned to let him see that his words had struck home. Looking disdainfully back at him, she said coldly: "You speak of Sir Gilroy as your enemy, yet but for him you would be lying prisoner in Newgate tonight. Is this how you repay him for saving your worthless life?"

The highwayman laughed. "He came to my aid to serve his own purpose," he said derisively, "and not through any concern for me. He desires nothing so much as my death, but would have it come about secretly. Too much would be made known if ever I stood trial."

Rowena continued to stare at him, anger rising within her to overwhelm both remorse and fear. More hints, more oblique references to some unworthy secret which this arrant rogue shared with Sir Gilroy. Suddenly she could endure it no longer.

"*What* would be made known?" she demanded imperiously. "Heaven defend me! I am weary unto death of these secrets and evasions. What knowledge do you possess, that Sir Gilroy will go to such lengths to keep it hidden?"

Colonel Fury looked startled, but surprise quickly gave way to amusement. He laughed, regarding her with frank approval. "By Heaven, madam, you do not lack spirit! I should have known that the woman Gil Mabyn chose for his bride would be no meek and timid creature." His glance flickered contemptuously towards Patience for a moment, and then returned to Rowena. He thrust back his chair and propped his feet on the table's edge, the ankles crossed. "So Gil keeps his own counsel, does he? That alone were reason enough for me to tell you what you desire to know!"

He paused, but Rowena continued to watch him as though fascinated. Dimly she was aware of her companions' suddenly quickened interest, of a feeling of suspense which gathered them all up and focused their whole attention on the man lounging at the head of the table, but now that the truth was about to be revealed she experienced an unexpected change of heart. She did not want to pry into Gil's secrets, to demand proof of his honesty. It was no longer important. The trust he had asked of her was his, completely and whole-heartedly, now that it might be too late to tell him so.

"On the night that I first found Mabyn here," Fury continued, "he was newly come from Warwickshire, where he had been visiting his sister, Beatrice." He paused, his sardonic glance resting upon Rowena's face, and then added deliberately: "Beatrice is my wife!"

Peter uttered an exclamation of astonishment, and Tobias and Patience exchanged a startled glance, but Rowena shut her eyes against the mockery in Fury's face, feeling shame and remorse as sharp as physical pain. His wife, Gil's sister! "I am concerned only to protect the innocent," Gil had told her, and she, believing that he lied, had flung the words back at him with spite and anger.

"That is the shameful secret Gil strives so valiantly to keep!" Fury's hateful, jeering voice continued. "It would deal a cruel blow to his pride if his sister's husband were revealed as Colonel Fury, and ended his days at Tyburn. That is the real cause of his concern, though I've no doubt *he* would like you to believe 'tis on her behalf alone, lest my execution leave her destitute. He knows that I would not seek death beneath the Press by refusing to plead, just to preserve my personal property for her." He laughed. "The more fool I, if I did! 'Tis years since I possessed any wealth save that which I take on the highway."

Against her will, Rowena listened to the callous words which made everything so abundantly plain. The cruel law by which the property of a convicted man was confiscated by the Crown left many families penniless, but it would scarcely mean actual hardship for the sister of a man as wealthy as Sir Gilroy. It was the shame of having her husband disclosed as so brutal a criminal as Colonel Fury which would be so unbearably hard, and bring added suffering into a life which must already have known a surfeit of it. She opened her eyes and looked again at the highwayman.

"If this be true," she said abruptly, "who are you? What is your name?"

At first it seemed that he was not going to reply, and then the broad shoulders lifted in a shrug. "Why should I not tell you?" he said carelessly. "The knowledge will avail you nothing. I am Kennet Falmer of Long Padworth in Warwickshire, sometime Colonel in the army of the late King. Does that content you?"

She stared at him, and then looked uncertainly towards her brother, who nodded. "That is the name of Gil's sister's husband," he said slowly, "but I supposed her a widow. 'Tis thus he speaks of her."

Fury laughed harshly. "That is what they would have the world believe," he said, "and if Gil had his way she would be a widow in very truth!"

There was a sound in the passage outside and Thomas entered the room again. "He be coming, Colonel," he said breathlessly. "He were riding hard when I first glimpsed him, but then he slackened pace and now comes on stealthily."

"Hoping to take me unawares," Fury added with a grin, "but I shall be ready for him." He swung his feet to the floor and got up, turning the chair so that it stood at right angles to the door instead of with its back to it. Then he came to grasp Rowena by the arm and haul her to her feet. " 'Tis on your account, I warrant, that he has ridden so fast from London. Sit there to greet him!"

He loosened her bonds and thrust her into the chair, fastening the ropes again so that she was held rigidly against the high back. Then he perched himself on the edge of the table facing her and signed to Thomas to take up a position beside the door, so that when it opened he would be hidden from view. The youth, thinking he could read his leader's purpose, grinned his understanding.

"Ye'll have me take him from behind, Colonel, as soon as he comes in?" he asked eagerly.

"No!" Fury's voice was cold. "I will do all that is needful."

He leaned forward and jerked at the fastening of Rowena's cloak, so that the silk-lined velvet slipped down and left her neck and shoulders bare above the low-cut satin bodice. Fury drew his sword and set its sharp point against her throat.

"Mabyn will offer no resistance," he said grimly, "neither will any here cry out a warning to him! Thomas, when I bid you, open the door, so that he may see the welcome I have prepared for him."

Rowena heard Tobias curse softly in anger at his own helplessness, but she dared not turn her head to look at him. Fury was sitting easily, one foot on the bench and his elbow resting on his knee, but she could feel the steel cold at her throat and knew that he would drive the blade home without hesitation if his own immunity were threatened.

The minutes dragged by with agonising slowness. If Gil had reached the inn he must have seen the light from the parlour shining through the cracks in the shutters, and be seeking entry at the rear of the house where all was in darkness, but Fury had foreseen this and taken measures to prevent it. The only point of access was the door which faced the track across the Heath.

At last came a stealthy footstep in the passage, the merest whisper of sound, yet loud enough to reach those who strained their ears within the parlour. Fury waited a moment longer and then gestured to Thomas with his free hand. Rowena heard the rattle of the latch, and the faint creak of hinges as the door swung slowly open.

"Sir Gilroy Mabyn, I believe?" Fury's tone was mocking, the words a sneering parody of those with which Gil himself had greeted him on a previous occasion in that room. "My dear sir, we have awaited your coming with all eagerness."

13

A Lady Defiant

There followed a long moment of silence and then Gil spoke, his voice low and even, yet charged with a consuming anger. "Damn you, Kennet!" he said. "Damn your black soul to Hell!"

Fury laughed. "Harsh words, Gil, but I will not hold them against you! Disarm him, Thomas, and bind him hand and foot. And be sure you make the bonds secure!"

Gil said no more as the command was obeyed, but Rowena could guess at the anger and frustration which must possess him, and once again she tasted the bitterness of vain regret. There would be no opportunity to make amends. Whatever the highwayman's intentions towards them might be, he dare not for his own sake premit them to escape.

At length Fury seemed satisfied. He sheathed his sword and stood erect, and Rowena, freed at last from the menace of the sharp steel, was able to look about her again. Gil, unarmed and bound, was sitting on the chest which stood against the wall opposite the window. Fury went across to him to assure himself that the ropes were securely tied, and for a moment or two blocked her view of the prisoner. Then he moved aside, and she looked across the room into Gil's eyes.

"I am to blame for this," she said with difficulty, "and I have no right to ask you to forgive me."

He smiled and shook his head. "Nor need to ask, either," he replied gently. "No doubt the fault was mine."

Fury gave a short laugh. "Gallant as ever!" he said with a sneer. "She has brought you to this, and you both know it!" He turned to Thomas, who stood silently awaiting his orders, Sir Gilroy's sword and sword-belt in his hand. "Your work here is done. Ride out and tell the other men they need keep watch no longer. Then go with them to the Green Man at Hatton and wait there for my coming. Take all the spare weapons with you." He took a purse from his pocket and tossed it across to the lad. "There's to drink my health!"

Thomas pocketed the gift with gleeful thanks and scurried off, and after a little while they heard him ride away. Rowena looked at those of her companions still within her range of vision. Tobias and Patience were behind her now, and because of the chair's high back she could not turn her head to look at them, but she could see Peter slumped in the corner of the other settle, his face grey with pain and exhaustion. His eyes were closed and he seemed on the point of collapse. Gil was watching the highwayman, who, with a freshly filled glass in his hand, had taken up a position with his back to the fireplace.

"All goes smoothly," Fury remarked with satisfaction, "and now but let my messenger come promptly to our meeting, and the last move may be made."

Gil looked about him. "I do not see Sir Daniel Hartland here," he said. "What has befallen him?"

"That which soon or late must befall us all," Fury replied callously. "He chose to play the hero, and met with a hero's customary reward."

"In plain words, you murdered him!" Gil spoke contemptuously, and glanced at the sword on the wall above the fireplace. "God's mercy, Kennet! do you never weary of killing?"

The highwayman's face darkened, his lips thinned to a hard, cruel line. "Were I never so weary, I would gladly bestir myself to make an end of you!" he said with sudden viciousness. "In the three years since I returned to the highway I have never stopped a coach without hoping to find you within it, nor ridden out without wondering how soon the day would come which would see you delivered into my hands." He paused, and slowly his expression changed to one of evil satisfaction. "Now it has come at last, and brought me not only you, but also your chosen bride, and I do not begrudge one of the weary months of waiting."

"Do you suppose I have not sought a meeting also?" Gil replied coldly. "I swore to kill you, Kennet, when I discovered how you had misused my sister, but by that time you had disappeared. When Peter Buckland described Colonel Fury to me, and told me of this place, I thanked God that my search was over at last."

"Then it is true?" Rowena spoke in a whisper. "This man *is* your sister's husband? She is the innocent you sought to protect?"

"She, and her children!" Gil's voice was level, but

194

his glance never shifted from Fury's face. "Two little daughters, and a boy born half a year after his father deserted them. Did you know that you have a son, Kennet? Or, knowing, would you have cared at all?"

Fury laughed, a harsh sound of contempt. "What is another puling brat to me? I'll wager, though, that my brother was well pleased, since he can get no sons of his own. How it must gall him that he cannot disinherit me and make the boy his heir!" He broke off, and a gleam of comprehension came into his eyes. "I begin to understand! Now that I have provided him with an heir more to his liking than myself, you may kill me with his good will."

"To Sir Marley Falmer you are already dead," Gil replied curtly, "and have been ever since you left your family to shift for themselves. He paid your debts and took Beatrice and the babes into his own house, but he swore that you shall never cross its threshold again."

"As to that, we shall see!" Fury retorted, jeeringly. "If I can see any profit in it, my brother is likely to find me an uncomfortably active corpse. As for your sister, she is still my wife, nor will she be able in future to look to you for help. Your race, my friend, is run!"

There was no need for him to enlarge upon this threat. The indescribable venom in voice and look left no doubt of his meaning, and Rowena felt her skin prickle with dread. Death was waiting to claim them all, but in what guise would it come? To what lengths would Fury go to satisfy his hatred?"

"Not while I still draw breath!" Gil's voice brought her gaze back to him, and she found that he was no longer looking at Fury, but at her, his eyes bright as aquamarines in his dark face. "When you see me lying dead, Kennet, you may cease to reckon with me, but not before."

The words were addressed to Colonel Fury, but Rowena knew that they were meant also for her, to give her courage and bid her not lose hope, even though all seemed lost. And somehow they succeeded, if not in overcoming her fear, at least in enabling her to conceal it. She lifted her head and looked steadily back at him, and somehow even contrived to summon up a faint smile.

"Fine words," Fury said with a sneer, looking from one to the other, "but words are easily spoken. We shall see presently if you can match them with deeds."

He paused, lifting his head to listen, and in a moment they all heard it, the drumming sound of approaching hoofbeats. Fury grinned.

"The final guest!" he said with satisfaction. "He comes prompt to time."

The hoofbeats drew closer and closer, until they came to a halt before the inn. Fury took out his pistol and stepped into the passage, drawing the door shut behind him, and Rowena, still watching Gil, saw him strain suddenly against his bonds, exerting all his strength in an attempt to break them. But the ropes held firm and he relaxed again, looking across at her with a rueful shake of his head.

They heard Fury speak in greeting and another, rougher voice reply, and then he came back into the parlour, followed by a man whose gaunt, lantern-jawed face was made more unattractive still by a broken nose. The newcomer cursed in astonishment at sight of the prisoners, and then, as his glance fell upon Peter, recoiled a pace with an inarticulate sound of alarm and disbelief.

"Be easy, Jed! 'Tis no ghost you see but a living man, for all that he looks more dead than alive," Fury reassured him with a laugh. "Our friend Birley lied when he said that I had slain his daughter's gallant." He laid his pistol on the table and returned to his former position before the fireplace. "Did you meet with anyone as you came hither?"

Jed Hollett shook his head, still staring at Peter as though he could not believe his eyes. "Nay, for I rode straight across the Heath. I guessed ye'd be waiting for me."

"With all impatience," Fury agreed sardonically. "What news do you bring?"

Hollett pushed back his hat and scratched his head. "News in plenty, Colonel," he said hoarsely, "but whether it be good or ill is more'n I can tell. I went to Long Padworth as ye bade me, but they tell me the squire there be a babe not yet breeched. Sir Marley Falmer died nigh on a month ago."

There was a pause, a moment of growing tension while the significance of those words made itself felt. Even Peter became aware of it, and raised his head to look at the man who stood so still and silent before the empty hearth.

"So my accursed brother is dead," Fury said softly at last, "and I master of all that was his!" Slowly his eyes turned towards Gil, and then, stepping across to him, he struck him twice, very deliberately, across the face. "And you, you impudent young devil, sought to fob me off with a paltry five thousand pounds!"

Rowena cried out in protest and distress, but neither

197

man paid any heed to her. Gil shook his head dazedly, and lifted it to look up at Fury, who still stood threateningly over him. He was very pale, and there was a trickle of blood from the corner of his mouth.

"I would not have offered you a single groat," he said with bold contempt, "but Beatrice would have it so. It was beyond my power to convince her that as long as you lived, her son's inheritance would never be safe. In the end I let her have her way, but make no mistake, Kennet! Had you agreed to the bargain you should have had your gold, but I would have followed you to France and killed you there."

"I do not doubt it!" Fury turned away to stand beside the table, and Jed Hollett, who had been staring at him in open-mouthed astonishment, found his voice to say in tones of awe: "Be that the truth, Colonel? You be brother to the old squire as died?"

"Aye, and father to the brat said to have succeeded him," Fury agreed with a laugh. "A rare jest, is it not?"

" 'Tis a jest I'd be glad to have played upon me," Hollett replied frankly. "This Sir Marley Falmer were a rich man, wi' a fine house and broad lands and I know not what besides." He paused, staring at his leader, and a look of cunning and of avarice dawned in his eyes. "When ye ride home to claim it, Colonel, ye'll not be forgetting old friends, will 'ee?"

"Be sure that I shall not!" Fury was apparently unaware of the change in his henchman's manner. He picked up the bottle and looked to see how much remained in it. "There is enough wine here to drink a toast to my good fortune. Fetch another glass from the cupboard yonder."

With a grin, Hollett turned to obey him as Fury set the bottle down again. The highwayman's hand moved swiftly to the pistol he had placed on the table. He lifted it, and as Hollett opened the cupboard to peer within the shot crashed out, deafening in the narrow confines of the room. The other man stiffened for an instant and then slid to the floor, leaving the cupboard door swinging to and fro. Patience screamed, but Rowena, after one great gasp of horror, closed her eyes for a moment and braced her body hard against the chair, willing herself desperately to remain calm.

"A trick well worthy of you!" Gil's voice reached her faintly, as though he spoke from a great way off. "The poor fool should have known better than to turn his back upon Colonel Fury."

"Greed made him blind to danger," the highwayman replied indifferently, putting the smoking pistol down on the table again, "but I had no mind to have him battening upon me for the rest of my days. This way, however, he can still be of use to me."

"Of use to you?" Gil repeated scornfully. "A dead man?"

"Even so," Fury replied mockingly. "You heard him say that none saw him come here. When Thomas left this room there were six people in it. There must be six here when he returns."

To Rowena the words seemed meaningless, and yet a fear which she could not define began to take hold upon her. She looked at Gil and saw that he was watching Fury intently, a frown between his brows. The highwayman was looking consideringly about him.

"We have had very little rain of late, and the whole

countryside is as dry as tinder," he added after a pause. "No doubt this place will burn passing well."

Rowena stared at him, thinking that she must have misheard or misunderstood, but then a glance at Gil's face, its set lips and narrowed eyes, told her that she was not mistaken.

"So that is your damnable intention," he said in a low voice. "To burn the inn, and us with it!"

"And Colonel Fury also," the other agreed mockingly. "My men will be amusing themselves at the Green Man, and no one else is likely to be nearby. The fire will be left to burn itself out and Fury die here with the rest of you, while Sir Kennet Falmer rides home to claim his inheritance."

"You forget," Gil said quietly, "that Beatrice knows you for Colonel Fury."

"And you forget that she is my wife. No, my friend, Beatrice will not betray me. I shall make sure of that!" He tipped the last of the wine into his glass, and then flung the bottle from him to crash into the corner of the room. "Damnation, 'tis empty! I must needs find another to pass the time until I leave this place. I shall so order matters that I am well away from here before the flames take hold, but I want no risk of any of my men returning before the fire has done its work, and ruining all my plans by setting you free."

Looking at Gil, Rowena saw in his face for the first time acknowledgment of defeat. "Not while I still draw breath," he had said, but what could he do, what could any of them do, bound and helpless as they were? Then the full horror of what Fury had just said swept over her, and her gaze shifted to him in blank disbelief.

"God in Heaven!" she whispered. "You do not mean to leave us to burn alive?"

He had been standing, his hands thrust deep into the pockets of his velvet coat, watching Gil as though he could not savour too deeply this moment of triumph, but at her words he turned his head to look at her.

"With regret, Miss Buckland," he replied carelessly. "Where you are concerned, with very deep regret."

"No!" It was Gil who spoke, as though the words were torn from him by something stronger than his will. "Kennet, you cannot do so monstrous a thing! Kill us if you must, but in the name of pity do it quickly, for the others at least! What grudge do you bear them to condemn them to so terrible a death?"

"What, will you plead for them?" Fury's voice was charged with evil satisfaction. "Will you grovel and crawl to save your lady-love from the flames? That would be a memory to cherish for the rest of my days!"

Gil's compelling gaze held his. "I would do even that," he said steadily, "if I believed for one moment that I could trust you to keep your word."

"No!" Rowena spoke sharply, prompted by an impulse she scarcely understood. "Sir Gilroy, I beg of you, say no more! I will endure anything rather than see you debase yourself by pleading with such a creature as this."

Fury turned sharply towards her, astonishment and then anger passing swiftly across his face to give place to an ominous amusement. "Bold words, madam," he said jeeringly, "but reckless! You might tempt me to put them to the test." He moved towards her and bent to place a hand beneath her chin, forcing her face up towards his. "If you will not have Gil plead for you, will you do so for yourself?"

The hazel eyes blazed up at him from her white face. At that moment anger and disgust possessed her to such a degree that she was unaware of fear.

"Never!" she replied in a tone of searing contempt. "Never, do what you will!"

He laughed, his hand sliding down her throat and across her bare shoulder. "A challenge, is it?" he taunted her. "I have never refused one yet, nor have I ever received one which intrigued me more."

She strained against the ropes, trying to draw away from the importunate hand, and with the movement remembered for the first time the little knife hidden in the pocket of her gown. As she felt the weight of it against her thigh, a tiny tentative glimmer of hope sprang to life within her. If she could somehow provoke him into untying her, create an opportunity to free the others from their bonds, Colonel Fury might yet find the tables turned upon him. It was a remote chance, but the only one that offered.

"I counsel you to refuse the challenge," she replied, forcing into voice and look all the scorn at her command, "for it could bring you nothing but defeat. I say again, do what you will! You will never force *me* to plead for mercy."

"No?" The sneer deepened about the cruel mouth. "I would take a wager that I will. You have a spirit t'would amuse me to break."

"And you, sir, have a monstrous conceit of yourself!"

"Rowena, for the love of God!" Gil's voice was agonised. "You know not what you do!"

She smiled and shook her head. "Do I not? My dear, if I am to die tonight, what matter what goes before?"

"Enough of this!" Fury's voice was suddenly harsh with anger. "Do you suppose I allow any pert wench to flout me so? Death can be unconscionably slow in coming, madam, and we shall see whether you hold your head so high an hour from now."

He moved round to the back of the chair, and her heart leapt with triumph as she felt his fingers tugging at the ropes. As soon as her arms were free, and though it was agony to move them from their cramped position, she slid her hand into her pocket and closed her fingers round the handle of the knife. Then she thrust the chair backward with all her strength, and in the same movement, as though in mortal terror and seeking her natural refuge, sprang up and stumbled across the room to Gil. Flinging herself down beside him on the chest, she threw her arms about him and pressed her face against his sleeve, while under cover of that close embrace she hacked frantically at his bonds.

Fury cursed as the heavy chair crashed into him, and then thrust it aside to stride forward in pursuit, but Gil, quick to take advantage of the altered situation, swung his bound feet vigorously at the other man's legs. Taken unawares, Fury lost his balance and fell sprawling to the floor, but was on his feet again almost immediately, his face livid with anger, one hand clawing at his sword. It was half out of its scabbard before he recovered his self-control, but then he slammed the weapon back again and glared down at Gil.

"No," he said savagely, "that were too swift by far! You do not cheat the flames that way, either of you!"

He seized Rowena by the arm and dragged her away with such violence that the knife slipped from her grasp and dropped, unnoticed by Fury, on to the chest. She cried out as his fingers dug into her flesh, and he laughed, thrusting her back against the table.

"Your courage deserts you even faster than I expected," he sneered, "but you will cry louder yet, mistress, that I promise you!"

Rowena was suddenly overwhelmed by a rush of blind terror. She could see Gil straining desperately but without effect at the ropes she had tried to sever, and knew that her wild bid to save them all had failed. Now she was at the mercy of a man wholly without pity and goaded almost to madness by her deliberate scorn.

Fury moved closer to her, hiding Gil from her view, and she snatched up the only weapon to hand, the empty pistol lying on the table beside her. With her free hand she seized it by the barrel and struck out desperately at the highwayman's grinning face. She felt the blow strike home and his grip on her arm slacken, and wrenched herself free to dart towards the door. Dragging it open, she fled along the passage and out into the luminous silence of the night.

At first her panic-stricken flight carried her towards the trees where they had hidden the horses, but even as she ran she realised the futility of it. Fury would overtake her before she could untether the animals and scramble into the saddle, and even if he did not, there must be another horse in the stable. She would be obliged to follow the track, but he, with his knowledge of the country, could cut straight across the Heath to intercept her.

She heard his heavy footsteps coming in pursuit, and turned sharply to dart through the gateway leading to the garden, her one desire to keep out of his sight. The path leading to the back door of the inn skirted the group of outbuildings, and the door of one of them stood open, gaping upon pitchy darkness. Prompted by an unreasoning instinct of self-preservation which urged her to seek any concealment from the horror that pursued her, she slipped within and pressed herself into the farthest corner.

It seemed impossible that so simple a ruse would succeed, and it was with almost incredulous relief that she heard the pursuing footsteps slow and hesitate, as though Fury had halted to look about him. Then they began again, more slowly this time, and she knew that he must be searching for her through the garden and among the trees.

It could be only a matter of time before he reached her hiding-place, but she could not bring herself to leave its shelter and try to re-enter the inn, even though to do so while Fury was still seeking her outside might enable her to set her companions free. Reason told her that she should attempt it, but fear was stronger than reason and her trembling limbs refused to obey the promptings of her mind. Like a rabbit cowering in its burrow while a fox prowled without, she crouched in the darkest corner of the shed, paralysed by terror.

Somewhere nearby a pebble crunched beneath the weight of a booted foot, and Rowena pressed the back of her hand against her mouth to stifle a gasp of alarm, breathing a silent, hopeless prayer that her pursuer would but glance within and then pass by. Crouched on her knees in the shadows, she stared with dilated eyes towards the entrance, where the moonlight fell clear and bright across the open door, hanging drunkenly from a single hinge.

As she stared, she caught sight of something which made her heart lurch sickeningly with dismay. From the splintered edge of the door hung a fragment of pale satin, torn no doubt from her skirt as she darted in. To her horrified eyes the scrap of stuff seemed as flamboyant as a waving banner, pointing the way unmistakable to her place of refuge.

The footsteps sounded again, closer still, and a shadow fell across the weathered wood of the door, the shadow of a man with a drawn sword in his hand. A moment later he stepped on to the threshold, a dark shape of indescribable menace, and his free hand reached out to pluck the scrap of satin from where it hung. For a moment he held it between finger and thumb, and then let it fall and took a step into the shed.

14

Barren Victory

Rowena was numb and petrified by terror, but the thumping of her heart seemed to shake her whole body, and it seemed impossible that the sound of it would not reach to the man by the door. In those few seconds she plumbed the uttermost depths of despair.

"Rowena!" The deep voice, muted to a whisper, came softly to her ears. "Rowena, are you there?"

Gil's voice! The shock of it was so great, the relief so profound, that she thought she was about to swoon. She could not speak, but she must have made some sound, for he moved slowly forward until he all but stumbled over her, and her hands reached up to clutch piteously at his coat. He bent, and with his free arm raised her to her feet, holding her tightly and murmuring reassurance while she clung to him in wordless thankfulness.

"How come you here?" she whispered at last. "How did you get free?"

"Your doing, sweetheart!" he replied softly. "You had not time to cut through my bonds, but you weakened them enough for me to break them. As soon as I was free, I took the sword from the wall and came in search of you."

"And Colonel Fury?"

"Still seeking you, and so we must not linger here." He held her a little away from him and looked down into her face. It was too dark to see his expression, but his voice had altered, become compelling. "Listen to me, Rowena! We go now to find him, and as soon as I cross swords with him you must go into the inn and set the others free. Tobias first. He is the only one able to defend you if aught befalls me."

Though her terror had subsided, it had still not altogether left her, and now his words woke dread of another kind in her heart. Somehow she dissembled it and whispered her agreement, only adding, with a catch in her voice: "Ah, take care!"

"I will, be sure of that!" He bent his head to kiss her lightly on the cheek. "Now come!"

His arm still around her, he led her out into the open and along the path by which she had come. They had passed through the gateway and were almost at the inn door when Colonel Fury appeared from the direction of the stable. Gil's arm tightened for an instant about Rowena's shoulders and he said in a low voice:

"Remember what you must do!" Then, releasing her, he went quickly forward to meet his enemy.

The highwayman had stopped short at sight of them, cursing in furious astonishment. There was blood upon his face where the pistol-butt had struck him, but the wound seemed merely superficial, for as Gil moved towards him he unsheathed his sword, and the moonlight ran in a cold, blue-white gleam along the deadly blade.

With the vicious sound of sword against sword pursuing her, Rowena fled into the house. It needed all her resolution so to turn her back upon what was happening there on the open space before the inn, but she dared not disobey Gil again. Too often now she had seen the disastrous consequences of following her own headstrong inclinations.

In the parlour the three remaining prisoners waited in anguished suspense, and when Rowena entered, Patience gave a little cry of relief and Peter exclaimed: "Now God be thanked!"

Tobias, no less moved but practical as ever, said quickly: "Cut me loose, Miss Rowena, and let me see if that poor rogue yonder has a weapon about him. We'll not be taken unawares a second time!" As she snatched up the knife from where it lay and attacked the rope binding his arms, he added anxiously: "He did not harm you?"

She shook her head. "No, I hid from him, and then Sir Gilroy came." Her voice was unsteady with anxiety and distress. "They are fighting now outside."

"God grant Sir Gilroy victory!" Tobias said fervently, and Rowena's heart echoed the prayer with anguished intensity.

As soon as Tobias was free he stretched his cramped limbs and then moved quickly to where Jed Hollett lay huddled in the corner. A hasty search of the body yielded a serviceable pistol, and with this in his hand Tobias hurried out, leaving Rowena to finish releasing her brother and Patience. Peter tried to rise to his feet, but the ordeal had taken too great a toll of his strength and he reeled back on to the settle again, his face the colour of ashes.

With an exclamation of loving concern Rowena clasped him in her arms, holding him close in sudden anxiety. Patience, who had also stretched out her hands to help him, checked the movement and drew back. When Rowena looked up, the younger girl was standing with her hands tightly clasped at her breast, watching the brother and sister with stricken eyes.

The desolation in her white face smote Rowena with sudden remorse, and with the knowledge that Peter was no longer her own dearest concern. She rose quickly to her feet, putting out one hand towards her while with the other she signed to her to take her place at Peter's side.

"Care for him, Patience!" she said in a low voice. "That is *your* right."

She did not wait to see Patience obey her, but turned and went quickly from the room, drawn as though by a lode-stone to the spot where she had left Gil fighting with Colonel Fury. It was very quiet now, the clash of swords was silenced, and for a space dread held her prisoner in the darkness of the narrow passage before she could summon up the courage to face whatever awaited her beyond. Then, because for good or ill it must be faced, she stepped slowly forward into the doorway.

The barren, desolate Heath, patched with the dark shadows of tree and thicket, lay empty and forbidding under the indifferent moon, and a few yards away at the edge of the track, Tobias knelt beside the dark shape of a fallen man. Close by stood Gil, breathing heavily, the point of his sword resting on the ground.

Relief flooded over her, leaving her weak and trembling so that she had to clutch at the doorpost for support, while the scene before her shifted and wavered in a silvery mist. Then Gil turned and saw her standing there. He said something in a low voice to Tobias, and then handed him the sword and came to take Rowena's hands in his.

"It is over," he said quietly. "With God's help, and yours, I have done what I set out to do."

"*My* help!" she whispered. "Ah, do not mock me! Not at this time!"

"I do not mock, Rowena," he replied seriously. "But for you, not one of us would have lived to see another day. You are the bravest woman I have ever known!"

She shook her head, knowing that whatever courage she had shown had been born of sheer desperation, but his words sent a warm flood of pleasure through all her being. No compliment she had ever received had given her greater happiness.

Tobias came to join them and they went back into the inn, there to take counsel what next to do. It was plain that the most pressing need was to return to the safety of Hounslow, for though Fury had ordered his men to await his coming, it was possible that one or more of them might return. It seemed doubtful, however, whether Peter was in a fit state to ride so far.

"I will contrive!" he said stoutly when the doubt was voiced. "Patience and Rowena must not linger in this place." He leaned his head against the back of the settle and looked up at Sir Gilroy with a faint smile. "I charge you, Gil, if I show signs of flagging, to bind me to the saddle and lead my horse yourself."

Gil nodded. "As you will, Peter! I own I shall feel happier once the women—and the wounded also, for that matter—are placed in safety. Tobias, will you go fetch the horses? It will be best, I think, if Miss Hartland is mounted behind you."

As Tobias went briskly to do his bidding, Patience looked timidly up at Gil. "My father, sir?" she faltered. "I cannot—leave him thus!"

He was silent for a moment, regarding her with compassionate eyes. "I fear you must," he said gently, "for the needs of the living must come before those of the dead. He shall have proper and honourable burial. I give you my word upon that."

She hesitated, looking with troubled eyes from him to Peter. Rowena reached out sympathetically to take her hand.

"You must do as Sir Gilroy says, Patience, hard though it be," she said. "Come now, and let me help you to make ready!" She leaned forward and added in a whisper too soft for the men to hear: "For Peter's sake, my dear! See how ill he looks, in spite of his bold words."

Patience looked, and protested no more. She allowed Rowena to help her prepare for the journey, and then went quietly to the kitchen and knelt for a while in prayer beside her father's body. When she rose again she seemed to have achieved a measure of resignation.

By that time the horses had been brought, and Gil and Tobias had carried the body of Colonel Fury into the house. The door was secured and the little party mounted and rode away, leaving the inn of the Seven Magpies dark and silent in the cold light of the moon, tenanted only by the dead.

They rode in silence, each burdened with their own thoughts, and memories of that grim night, and so came at last to Hounslow, and the inn where the servants waited with the coach. Here Sir Gilroy once more took command, rousing the sleepy landlord and stirring him to such activity that food and wine were soon forthcoming, and rooms made ready for Peter and the two girls. Before they parted, Gil drew Rowena aside.

"Rest here till noon or thereabouts," he said quietly, "and then get you back to London so that Peter may have a physician's care. This night has taxed him more than he will confess."

She nodded, her brow puckering with anxiety as she glanced at her brother. "And you, sir?"

"I must remain to set matters in order here. Tobias had best stay with me, if you will give him leave."

"Of course, if you so desire it!" She paused, waiting for him to speak again, but he said no more. After a moment she turned away, and went with Patience to the bedchamber they were to share.

He was gone from the inn by the time she rose again, and had not returned when they set out for London. Peter declared that the few hours' rest had completely restored him, but there was a brightness in his eyes and a flush in his hitherto pallid cheeks which caused Rowena and Patience to exchange glances of misgiving and concern. The journey seemed endless, and anxiety for her brother left little room in Rowena's mind for anything else.

When at last they reached home she found herself fully occupied in allaying the curiosity of Mrs. Marriott and the servants, giving orders for Peter's comfort, and looking after Patience, whose uncertainty and timidity caused her to cling as closely to Rowena as any shadow. Rowena, herself driven to the uttermost extreme of weariness, kept her temper with an effort and wished that Tobias were there to help her shoulder the burden.

He returned the following day, grey-faced with fatigue but with reassuring news to tell. Sir Gilroy had concocted a tale to account for the circumstances of Colonel Fury's death, though it was a story which would not have withstood close examination. As he had expected, however, the local Justices were so relieved to find themselves rid at last of the notorious highwayman that they had refrained from questioning their deliverer too closely. The secret of Fury's identity would go with him to the grave.

Rowena received Tobias alone, for Peter was still confined to bed, and his sister had had the happy thought of sending Patience to sit with him. Mrs. Marriott, who had gladly taken the girl under her wing, had gone with her for the sake of propriety.

"What of Sir Daniel Hartland?" Rowena asked when Tobias had come to the end of his story.

"He is to be buried as Silas Birley," Tobias replied, "and Mistress Patience will bear that name until she is wed. Sir Gilroy believes 'twill be better so!"

After a moment's thought Rowena agreed. Sir Daniel Hartland had passed from the knowledge of the world fifteen years before, and to recall him would be to open old wounds, rouse long-dead bitterness. Better for Patience to come to her new life free of the burden of the tragic past.

"And Sir Gilroy?" she asked after a pause. "Did he return to London with you?"

"Aye!" Tobias regarded her with a shrewdness which penetrated her assumed indifference. "But you need not look to see him yet awhile. He has scarcely slept at all these two days past."

She made some careless rejoinder and sent him away before going to tell Peter and Patience the news he had brought. She expected Gil to visit her next day, but as the hours slipped past and he did not arrive, she began to grow anxious. Was it possible that the happenings of the past week had had repercussions which none of them had foreseen?

By the following morning, anxiety had reached a pitch where she felt compelled to send Tobias to make discreet inquiry at Sir Gilroy's lodging. She waited impatiently for his return, but when he came he brought news which filled her with indignation. Sir Gilroy had not been at home, but his servants said that all was well with him. If Tobias's business with him brooked no delay, they believed that he would find him at Whitehall.

The news that Sir Gilroy had considered attendance at Court more important than calling upon her immediately caused Rowena to regret her anxiety, and to regret even more her betrayal of it. She dismissed Tobias, and spent the next half hour debating what she would say to Sir Gilroy when at length he deigned to visit her, but it seemed that this was labour lost. Time passed, and still he did not come.

Peter was now well enough to leave his bedchamber, and he and Patience were absorbed in plans for the immediate future. Since it would not at present be possible for him to take his bride to Court, he proposed an early return to Mereworth, and desired Mrs. Marriott to go also in order that she might guide and instruct Patience in the management of a large household. Rowena supposed that she was also included in these arrangements, but she was neither informed of it nor consulted as to her own wishes, and an unpleasant sensation of being slighted added itself to her already ruffled feelings.

As soon as they had dined, she withdrew ill-humouredly to her bedchamber to brood over her wrongs, and found her thoughts returning most frequently to the shortcomings of Sir Gilroy Mabyn. It was obvious, she decided, that her first judgment of him had been the correct one, and not that formed under the stress of their recent adventures.

At last restlessness drove her back to the parlour, and she was surprised to find Mrs. Marriott sitting there alone. The widow regarded her with equal astonishment.

"Why, cousin, what do you here?" she exclaimed. "I supposed you with your brother and Miss Birley in the library, for Sir Gilroy has been closeted with them there this past half hour!"

"Sir Gilroy here?" Rowena's indignation struggled with astonishment. "Why was I not informed? Does Patience Birley count herself already mistress of this house?"

Mrs. Marriott, realising that her innocent remark had sparked off an anger out of all proportion to the fault, sought in alarm to soothe it. She did not succeed, and when presently a servant came in to say that Sir Gilroy desired Miss Buckland to receive him, Rowena turned on him in a rage.

"Since Sir Gilroy chooses to wait upon me only as

an afterthought," she said angrily, "you may tell him that I do not choose to receive him—now or ever!"

"Give yourself the satisfaction, madam, of telling him so yourself." Gil's voice replied in a tone of lazy amusement, and he came past the startled footman into the room. Bowing to Mrs. Marriott, he said courteously: "Madam, your servant! With your leave I would speak privately with Miss Buckland."

The widow glanced from him to Rowena's stormy countenance and came to the conclusion that they would do better alone. She had no desire to be a witness of the quarrel which was evidently brewing.

When she had gone, Gil closed the door behind her and turned back to Rowena, who cast him a darkling glance.

"Was it necessary, sir, to force your way into my presence?"

He laughed. "Certainly, since you did not intend to receive me. I will own that I hoped for a somewhat kinder reception."

"Indeed, sir? When you have been so tardy in coming?"

He shrugged. "There has been a deal to do. The affair of Colonel Fury, you know, did not end when we rode away from the inn."

"I am aware of it! What I did not know was that it needed to be settled at the Palace of Whitehall."

He came slowly towards her, laughter still lingering in his eyes. "So that rankles, does it? I went to Court because there was too much speculation afoot concerning my sojourn in Newgate. It might have led to disclosures which none of us desire. It was necessary to put an end to it before it spread beyond our control."

This was reasonable enough and it mollified her a little, but there still remained his neglect of her that day. She said indignantly: "Why was I not told earlier that you were here? Surely whatever you had to say with regard to Colonel Fury concerned me as well as Peter and Patience?"

"I came to return to Patience her father's sword, and to tell her of the arrangements I have made for his burial. She will wish to visit his grave before Peter takes her to Leicestershire. It did not seem that these matters would be of interest to you, and what I do have to say to you is for your ears alone." He paused, but even as she wondered what he meant by that, he added with a searching look: "Are you reconciled yet to the prospect of Peter's marriage? You know that it will mean estrangement from him if you are not?"

She nodded and turned away, her annoyance with him lost for a moment in graver matters. "She can never be the bride I would have wished to see him choose, but I cannot prevent their marriage, and I love him too well to quarrel with him over it. I pity her, and perhaps in time I may even grow to like her."

"I trust that you will, for her sake and your own." He paused, and when he spoke again there was a subtle change in his voice. "And your own marriage, madam? Are you reconciled to that?"

She did not reply at once. She knew the answer to the question well enough in her heart, and had he asked it that night at the Seven Magpies she would have given it without hesitation, but now she was less sure. The man who had shared with her the perils of the lonely inn seemed to have vanished, and to this courtier with the mocking eyes she could confess nothing of what she felt. To do so would be to humiliate herself beyond measure.

"I must learn to be so, it seems," she said at length. "Peter insists upon it, and I have no choice but to obey."

His brows lifted in pretended surprise. "I did not realise that you stand in such awe of your brother. Or that he would force you upon any course truly repugnant to you."

This was true, and they both knew it. Fortunately there was yet another way of saving her pride.

"He would not, but neither will he give his consent to any other match. I have no desire to remain a spinster sister in the house of which Patience is mistress."

"So I am the lesser of two evils!" Gil sounded more amused than angry. "I am flattered, of course, but I believe that a happier solution to the difficulty presents itself."

"Oh?" Hitherto Rowena had deliberately avoided his eyes, but at that her glance lifted, surprised and a little mistrustful, to meet his. "What is that, sir?"

"Some men," he replied reflectively, "see nothing amiss in taking an unwilling bride, but I am not one of them. You say that Peter will give his consent to no other match, but if I withdraw my claim to your hand, he will do so readily enough." His clear, compelling gaze held hers, and there could be no doubt of his sincerity. "Your freedom, Rowena! I love you well enough to make you a gift of it!"

She stared unbelievingly at him, hearing the words

yet not accepting them, feeling the world crumble into fragments and leave her lost and bewildered. The prize she had fought for and striven after for so many months had been placed in her hands, only to shatter like a pricked bubble, so that she clutched at emptiness.

Gil stood watching her for a moment, but when she did not speak he bowed and turned away. He had reached the door before she woke from her stunned disbelief to recognise the barrenness of victory and the folly of empty pride.

"Gil, wait!" She spoke breathlessly as she went quickly towards him, unaware that in the stress of the moment she had addressed him by his shortened name and without the formality of his title. "You mistook my meaning! I am not unwilling to marry you."

He halted and turned to face her, and as she paused before him she felt thankful for his great height, since it made it easier for her to avoid his eyes. As she stared fixedly at the costly lace of his cravat, she heard him say softly:

"Why? Because I offer the easiest way of escape from giving place to Patience?"

She shook her head, nervously clasping and unclasping her hands, but could find no words with which to answer him. The silence seemed to stretch unbearably, and still she could not bring herself to speak.

"Why?" he said ruthlessly. "Tell me, Rowena!"

"Because I love you!" Unexpectedly temper came to her aid, giving her the courage to lift her eyes to meet his. "You plague me and bully me, and say that I am spoiled and headstrong, but, Heaven protect me, I love you!"

She saw the ready laughter leap into his eyes again, but now there was something behind the laughter, a deeper flame which woke in her an instant response. He caught her in his arms and held her so, looking down into her face.

"At last!" he said in a low voice. "By Heaven, sweetheart, I feared you would never admit it!"

She gasped, but he kissed her before her indignation could find expression in words. When at length she did have an opportunity to speak, she said breathlessly:

"You tricked me into confessing it! Why, if you were so certain of it yourself?"

"Coxcomb I may be," he replied with a laugh, "but I was *not* certain! And I wanted to be, Rowena! I wanted to know beyond all doubt that you would marry me because you loved me, and not to please Peter or to avoid taking second place to Patience. The only way I could win you was by letting you go."

"What if I had not confessed it?" she persisted. "What then, sir?"

"I would have kept my word, and made no further claim upon you. I am a gambler, love, and always will be, though never before have I staked so much upon a single throw!"

She laughed and shook her head at him in mock reproof, although her heart failed her as she realised how nearly her obstinacy and pride had parted them. Had she let him go, he would not have returned, for though he loved her it would not change his nature, any more than her love for him would change hers. Their life together would be a stormy torrent rather than the placid, smooth-flowing stream of which she had once dreamed, yet as she looked up into his gipsy face and laughing, challenging eyes, she knew that she turned from peace to turbulence gladly, and without regret.